WISE WOMAN'S TELLING

Book One
in the sequence
Daughter of Tintagel

WISE WOMAN'S TELLING

Book One
in the sequence
Daughter of Tintagel

Fay Sampson

HEADLINE

First published in 1989
by HEADLINE BOOK PUBLISHING PLC

Reprinted in this edition in 1990
by HEADLINE BOOK PUBLISHING PLC

British Library Cataloguing in Publication Data

Sampson, Fay, *1935–*
    Wise woman's telling.
    I. Title
    823'.914 [F]

ISBN 0-7472-0220-6

Printed and bound in Great Britain by
Richard Clay Ltd, Bungay, Suffolk

HEADLINE BOOK PUBLISHING PLC
Headline House,
79 Great Titchfield Street
London W1P 7FN

To Jack

Author's Note

In physics, Dark Matter forms an unseen world that is the inverse of the matter we observe. The two were created to exist in equal proportions. Together they hold the universe in balance. But when they come into contact, the result is mutual destruction. Morgan's story is the Dark Matter of Britain.

The name Tintagel, formerly believed to be Norman, may be much older and Cornish. If so, it should be pronounced with a hard g. One possible meaning is 'the strong place where the two currents meet'.

The Tintagel of legend is a fortress, the birthplace of Arthur and the seat of King Mark of Cornwall. The archaeologists who excavated it believed that in Arthurian times it was in fact a Celtic monastery. Others have challenged this. The headland was certainly occupied in the fifth century, but as yet there is no conclusive evidence of its function.

The Western Sea

The Sisters

The Convent of the White Nuns

Tintagel Haven

Barras Nose

Tintagel Island

The Mother's Hole

The grave of Gorlois

To Padstow

To Dimilioc

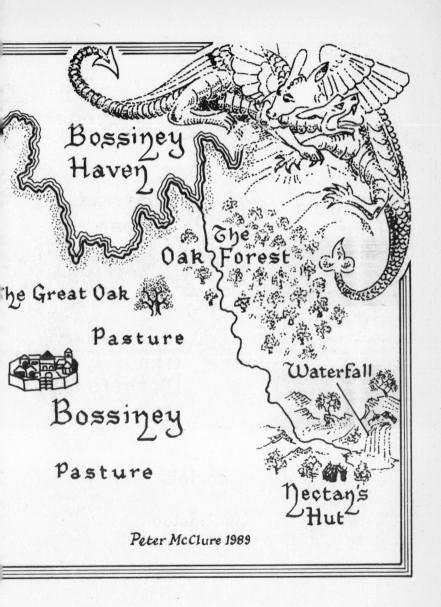

Bossiney Haven

The Oak Forest

The Great Oak

Pasture

Bossiney

Pasture

Waterfall

Nectan's Hut

Peter McClure 1989

Chapter One

It was the worst thing we ever did when we forgot Morgan, that night above all nights. Many's the time I've wept for it since. And that's nothing to the harm that will come of it yet.

And such a night it was. The gale screeching like the Black Hunt across the sky, and the sea howling up at us out of the caves around Bossiney Haven. And the rain! I can feel the cold of it stabbing into my joints to this very day. You'd have thought the Mothers' own waters had broken in the heavens above and they were all three of them screaming in labour.

But I couldn't close the door and get to bed. Not that night. Every door and window had to stand open, never mind the rain, and every knot let loose. There mustn't be anything closed or tied 'til the baby was safely born.

So I sat in that cruel draught, with my thighs wide open to the night, and holding the lips of my own blood-hole apart, though it had been dry these many years. Easy, easy, I was grunting. I was casting the spells of opening, and at the same time heaving and groaning, just as if I was bringing the child I'd never had into the world.

Morgan wasn't the only one they'd forgotten, my Lady Ygerne and her fine Uther Pendragon, that liked to call himself King of all the Britons. In Gorlois's time she'd have wanted me beside her, where I'd been when her three daughters were born. It was my craft she'd have trusted to bring her and the baby home through it then, never mind the midwife. But Gorlois was dead, and I was out of favour. Maybe King Uther thought I was only good for getting girls.

That's all Morgan was to him, that strutting fool of a man. A little girl. The youngest of Lord Gorlois's brood of daughters. But he should have known better, after what he'd seen. Only nine she might be, but he could hardly pretend she was too young to understand what had happened to them all. Though in fairness none of us guessed what was in her mind even then, though we found out soon, to all our cost.

Nine months they had been forgetting Morgan, King Uther Pendragon and his new queen, Ygerne. Queen before her husband's body was cold in the grave and the worms had hardly begun to nibble his parts. Nine months those two had petted and pawed each other for everyone to see, though not so much lately as they had done at first. Well, not on her side, anyway. But that didn't stop Uther Pendragon from having his pleasure wherever he could find it. And now her time had come, her hour of reckoning for that first night that broke Morgan's heart, and the lamps were burning late in our queen's bower. They were busy now. We could see shadows passing before the light. The baby was pushing to be born.

And all this time that little maid Morgan stood in the doorway with her wet face turned to the storm, and there was nothing I could do to shift her.

'Come away in, my lover,' I begged. 'You'll catch your death of cold, and it will be my back that pays for it with a beating, not yours. Tomorrow will be bad enough as it is, me crippled up with the rheumatism

2

already, and sitting with my feet in a puddle like a leaky boat, without having you ill as well. Come to bed now, there's a good maid, and snuggle under the blankets.'

She never even heard me. I could only see her back. Still, she was. You would have thought she was life-less, like a storm-struck tree. Hour after hour she'd stood, with her face to the rain and the lights and the bustle. And never a word she spoke or a muscle stirred. But she was living, all right. I could feel a spirit buried inside her that made the rest of the world seem half dead. It made me afraid, I can tell you.

I am an old woman now and I wasn't so young even then, for I had been nurse to Morgan's two sisters that were grown girls, and to their mother before that. Those two were lying there in the darkness under the furs. I could tell Elaine was sleeping because she was snoring like a pig, though before another year had turned she might be sweating and straining with a baby of her own. Pretty and plump and pink she was, and no trouble to any of us. Though not so innocent as she looked, either. She could see further than most. She was always her mother's favourite, and the queen had whispered her what she knew. Mother to daughter. Woman to her own blood. But I had no daughter of my womb. Or son, either.

So it made me cross, hearing her snoring. Young though she was, she could have helped me a little if she'd wanted to, and Margawse too, though that one was newer in the knowledge than Elaine. It was their own mother in pain, wasn't it? But there, they were neither of them wives yet, and it was no work for maids. And they'd no more call than Morgan to help the Pendragon's child into the world.

It was Margawse now who lifted her head. She

cried, 'What's the matter? Is something wrong? Has she dropped the baby yet?'

I could smell the excitement strong on her, like a soaked breech-cloth, and I thought, not for the first time either, that it was time she was married and away from that place. The eldest, Elaine, was betrothed already to King Nentres. Uther had seen to that. A handsome queen she'd make. And a wise one too, if you take my meaning. Margawse had come to her womanhood only lately, with no father of her own. And that was a dangerous thing for all of us. I had seen her up against a wall with Uther Pendragon, that day in the treasury. He wasn't the man – for all he called himself a Christian king – to care that he was married to her mother now. He took what he wanted, as we had cause to know. And Margawse was not the maiden to say no – if maiden indeed she was, which I very much doubted.

But what was I to do? Those girls were too head-strong for me. And their mother's head was so turned she couldn't see anyone but the king. Yet they called her a wise woman, Ygerne. And I should know, for it was not her own mother that had the whispering of that one. It's not every peasant woman can claim a queen for her daughter, by the Mothers' blood. They say it was Merlyn brewed the spell that tricked her, and I don't doubt he did, but in a man's world it's the man's story the bards tell. I've often wondered if there was more to it than that. Of course, I wasn't there when she went to the king's fine court, my little Cornish lady. But when she and my Lord Gorlois came galloping home with the king hard on their heels, there was more than a little look of Margawse in her face. She wasn't ill-pleased with herself. And why the king should be so hot after her, when he could

have had any lady in Britain for the asking, it's not for
me to tell. She never went high in our mysteries. Not
as high as me, if I do boast. Still, she did know enough
for that. And she wanted to be loved. She wanted a
son. Best of all, she wanted a son that might be king.

But she and her daughters had slept in Tintagel on
a terrible night, when the spirits were abroad. And in
those days Tintagel was a women's place. Merlyn
wove his own magic, oh, yes! But it's my belief that
under the rock the Mothers were laughing at the lot of
us. And true it is that none of us have been the same
since that time.

So the night went on, cold-footed as a toad, and
Margawse fell back to grumbling.

'I'm freezing. Give me another cover, Gwennol. I'll
die soon.'

'You've had every one there is. There's only this old
blanket I've got about my shoulders, and I'm not giving
you that. I'm as damp as a ditch in February, as it is,
and lucky to live 'til then, sitting here shivering with
the door open and the bed-chamber like a bog.'

'Make Morgan come to bed then. Or shut the door
and leave her outside.'

She knew I couldn't shut any opening 'til the baby
was born. But she didn't care.

I was past arguing with either of them. I was too
damp and cold and tired even to move my jaws. My
head was so heavy, I'd have given a month of my life
to lay it down and sleep. But I had power to use for a
birthing, even for those that didn't want it now. I
could still show them. And then, I daren't leave
Morgan to watch alone. Only nine years old she was,
and there wasn't one of us could bend her to our will.
Not even if we had beaten her. Least of all then. Her
father was gone and he was the only one that she'd

5

ever let touch her. There was nothing any of us could do for her but wake and watch. And there was no one left to do it but me. Her father was dead, and her mother had forgotten her.

But I'll swear to this. I had never whispered Morgan, not so much as a word. Not then. That was her mother's place. A year before she'd bespoken Elaine, and then Margawse, when Uther Pendragon was coming. But never Morgan. To tell you the truth, my lady was more than a little frightened of Margawse and Morgan, her own daughters. But for all I believed her, I knew there was power in that child already. And when I think how it must have come to her, through no human being, it makes my hair creep sometimes.

A gust of wind slammed the door back against the wall. It blew a stink of wet wool and leather across my face. I shuffled back, trying to get out of the draught. But Morgan never moved, though the gale was dashing rain into her eyes and there was black water swilling about her feet.

An ugly, drenched scrap of a thing she was. As thin and draggled as a black kitten that's just been born. To see her like that you would never have thought she would have grown into a beautiful queen. Margawse now, you couldn't miss her, with her red hair and her skin like buttermilk. Or Elaine, that everyone said was the prettiest of the three, though I never saw much in her myself. But Morgan had always been a strange maid. 'Like a crow in a thunderstorm,' Uther Pendragon said when he first set eyes on her. Yet she had a way with men when she wanted to. The way she used to smile at her father.

And then I caught sight of something fluttering, pale as moths in the darkness, down Morgan's skirt. I

peered closer and then I let out a scream. Her little
hands were twisting her girdle, tying it tight, knot
after knot, over and over. No wonder that baby was
slow in coming.

'You little black witch!'

The words were out of my mouth before I knew
what I was saying. I tore her crooked fingers from the
cord and tugged out those cruel knots 'til the whole
thing fell free. I felt those tight cramps in my belly
moving loose and I could breathe deep and strong
again. She didn't try to stop me. Just laughed at me
with her little white teeth, though never a sound she
made.

Well, I daren't take my eyes off her after that,
though it made them swim, peering through that
murk. I was nearly crying from the fire in my joints
and the icy cold in my feet. Then Morgan let out a
gasp that was almost a shriek. In spite of my rheumatism I was in that doorway as fast as I could move,
never mind the mud squelching under my feet. She
clutched at my dress with the bones of her skinny
white hands.

'Is it born, Gwennol? Is it here?'

We heard Queen Ygerne cry out louder than the
scream of the wind, and there was a thin high wail
through the rain and the darkness. He had come. The
baby was born alive.

For a moment I forgot Morgan. I am an old woman
that never bore a child. Any woman's baby starts a
hunger in me, and a queen's baby is more precious
than most. And if what I guessed about Ygerne was
true, then in a way that child came partly from my
doing. Almost my own blood it felt. Then I remembered Morgan. I looked down to see how she was
bearing it – and she was gone. I'll swear it was only a

7

moment I forgot her. But I had lost her, like a black cat in the darkness.

Then someone lifted the curtain. I saw the queen's bed, gold in the candlelight. A woman ran out, shouting to us all, 'It's a boy!' And there was Morgan, running towards the light, with her skirt sticking to her knees.

A shadow came between her and the doorway. I can see it now. A man's shadow. You couldn't mistake the shape of big Uther Pendragon, striding into my lady's bedchamber. We saw his shadow huge across the curtain. He was like a giant bending over the bed. Over his wife and son, that should have been the wife and son of Gorlois, Morgan's father. We saw him lift that golden child in his arms before the door slammed shut.

A boy. And Gorlois's little maid was left outside in the dark and the storm. He never even noticed her.

'Morgan!' I cried, though I could hardly hear myself for the wind. I knew it would be no use. She had gone. What hope had I got of catching her, old and stiff as I was, and the rain fit to wash us all out to sea? I knew what she was going to do, poor little scrap, for child she was still, and could still be hurt. She would make her body suffer 'til it was as bitter as her soul. She'd gone beyond my help now. The darkness had taken her. And we may all suffer for that.

Chapter Two

She was happy once, in her own way. Though it seems
so long ago now that I sometimes wonder if I didn't
dream it.

It was only her father she loved. He had the power
to swing her off to the Blessed Isles with one hug of his
big strong arms about her. And the same power to
hurt her. Like a puppy that hasn't got the sense to get
out from under its master's feet. She could be sharp
with her teeth like a puppy too, but she'd come crawling back as if she was wagging her little tail and
begging him to love her again. That was a bitter lesson
she had to learn: to make herself be loved and not to
love back. There isn't a woman in Britain has learned
it better.

It was hunting that her father loved best. So nothing would satisfy Morgan but she must go with him.
She was riding into the forest with the hunt almost as
soon as she could sit. When other little maids were
crawling about the floor playing with dolls, Morgan
would be out with the men. I remember the day she
came back, her face smeared with blood and her eyes
shining like the dew on May-Morning. That was her
first kill. I warned her father then.

In those days one of the huntsmen would carry her
on his saddle in front of him. Not Gorlois, of course. If
she had been a son he might have done. But my lord

9

was too proud a spearman to slow his horse or spoil his aim for the sake of a scrap of a girl-child. It was enough for her that he let her follow him. She would twist her fingers in the horse's mane and crouch down low, as if she was whispering in his ears and urging him on faster.

My lady and Morgan's two sisters, now, they'd ride in the greenwood if the sun was shining. Sidesaddle, like the fine ladies they were – or wanted to be. And the ponies tricked out with bells and baubles that you'd have thought would have frightened every hare and deer for miles around, so loud they jingled. And their gowns and their skirts spread over the horses' rumps so that the light would catch the silken embroidery and the gold. And you can't go dashing under branches and through briars like that without tearing your gay gowns to shreds and messing your pretty hair.

But Morgan, now, she would hunt in any weather. Though if I'd been her mother I wouldn't have let her. But who would listen to old Gwennol? I was just their old nurse, too slow in the joints and too quick with her tongue. By daylight, anyhow. True, I had a name for a powerful skill with charms, but that was no more than women's medicine, or so the men thought. I didn't want Gorlois to know any different. But my lady did, for all her fine airs. She ought to have listened to me then. She'd heeded me once, when she was younger, or she wouldn't be called wise now.

Morgan was eight summers when her father let her hunt on her own pony. I saw them set off that day. She was gripping it between her knees that were as white as two peeled hazel wands, and not much thicker. Riding astride, she was, like a boy, with the skirt of her dress tucked up so high on her thighs it was hardly decent, even for a child so small, with all those men around. But that summer there was never a thought of such a thing in her little mind. Why should there be? It came to her too soon as it was, and from those that should have watched over her to keep her from harm. She'd have worn breeches like a boy then, if I'd have let her. She knew she was all the son her father would ever have. But she was never anything like a boy. She was too fey for that.

I watched them go, with the hounds and the horns and the spears tossing in the sunlight. And my heart was heavy with fear for her. I was twisting my apron between my hands like fishermen's mothers when they stand on the beach, watching the boats fighting their way back to harbour against a gale. But she was laughing, and her father with her. That great, black-bearded spearman and his little black-braided daughter. A giant with a dwarf. Well, they always say giants are stupid. It would be enough for me if he brought her safely back to us.

The hunt turned their backs on the sea and the sunlight, and rode in under those great branches of the oak forest. All their brave colours and bright harness were swallowed up in that old twilight. Hours, they could be lost before anyone caught a sight of them again, except for what lived there. That made me shudder. Gorlois didn't know the half of it. There's places there, old pools and bogs and circles of standing oaks, I wouldn't go near even in daylight without strong spells to guard me. There's times and seasons for places like those, and a right way of coming to them if you want to get away again with your life and your wits. And often as I have been, I'd never have had the courage 'til I'd drunk that cup that makes me more than old Nurse Gwennol when the moon is up.

So I wondered how long it might be before I'd catch a glimpse of them again, up on the clear ridge where the road runs past to Padstow. And it wouldn't be the first time if they came out of that forest fewer than they went in.

We women were left in Bossiney. It was a pleasant enough place – a clutter of houses, a hall big enough for a hundred warriors, and a wall round them. That's all it was then, before the king moved in. Bright sea and sky in front of us, black woods behind. It wasn't that Gorlois didn't have stronger forts in higher places, but what would have been the point in living up there and making ourselves more uncomfortable than we had to? They'd made him Duke of Cornwall, hadn't they? Leader of all their war-hosts. Who had he to fear this side of the Tamar?

But I had plenty to worry about, even if he hadn't. And worse to me than any Saxons.

All day I feared and fretted. Margawse screamed at me for a clumsy idiot when I tugged a tangle of the red hair clean out of her scalp with the comb. I dropped a jug of milk, and trailed my skirt through the fire so we almost had the hall in flames about our ears. And all the time my ears were listening for the horn and my eyes watching for the first horses breaking out of the trees.

Like the little luck-cat she was then, she came back from it alive, and laughing as if she had been in paradise. And her knife still covered in blood.

Her father was mightily pleased with her too. I could see that, and for once I was glad for her. He rode up beside her, his big horse towering over her little pony, and he clapped his hand on her shoulder so hard that she almost fell under the blow.

'Well, Gwennol, what do you think of that? She's

galloped all the way across the Alan and up to Caer
Delinuth, hunting the biggest boar I've seen in a
twelvemonth. And she came in at the last in time to
have her knife in his side with all the others, before
he'd done squealing. Look, she's got his ear to show
you. A boy couldn't have done much better on his first
ride.'

He grinned and hugged her to him, and she smiled
at him, so happily, it made my heart turn over to
watch it. I've never had a child smile at me like that,
for all I've nursed so many and broken my heart over
one of them. But it's not the same as your own.

I suppose that made me a little sharp.

'Poor lamb! Just look at her. She's almost dead with
weariness. We'll have her in bed for a month before
she's fit to ride again.'

And I wasn't far from the truth, for she must have
driven herself as hard as a grown man. When he took
his great hand away from her shoulder, she fairly fell
into my arms off her pony, and it was all I could do to
hold her upright and set her safely on her feet.

The gown she'd kilted up fell back to her feet, all
ripped and splattered with mud as it was. And when
she put up her hand she couldn't stop it from shaking
now. She picked off the ribbon I'd braided her hair
close against her neck with, so she shouldn't hang
herself in the forest. She always hated to be bound,
and she shook her black hair free.

He saw her then for what she was. A drooping little
girl, filthy, tired out, and never as strong in health as
any of us would have wished. He knew she could
never be the son he wanted. He swore by names I'd
never heard him use and didn't think he knew, and he
turned his back on her. He flung himself from his
horse and strode off to his wife, all splashed with

13

blood as he was. And it wasn't love he'd be pushing himself into her for.

Poor, foolish man. I knew what drove him, while I picked my baby up in my arms. He was praying that Morgan wouldn't be the last child he spawned. And I saw by the look in her eyes as they followed him that she knew what he was thinking too.

Chapter Three

Summers end in killing-time, when the scythe's in the corn and the hare hides herself in the last stand 'til the reaper throws his sickle at it and there's blood in the stubble.

We drank the harvest home, and those that hadn't got their bellies big at May-time had another go. But we were hardly sober before those whetstones were shrieking again, and it wasn't sickles they were brightening this time. The men were off to war again.

I've never seen a Saxon. Summers come and summers go, like the tides in a cove. You don't expect the world to change. The sea's not going to come pounding in and then refuse to stop. It's not going to come flooding up the coombes and washing into our duns to sweep us all away, is it? There's spring tides and neap tides, full moon and dark. What has been will come again. There's a pattern to everything. Cornwall was like a high ground we'd built on. I couldn't think that those Saxons might just keep marching west and never stop until they crossed the Tamar. Every flood comes to its top and flows back.

Summer after summer it had been going on, the gentry riding out on their brave little horses, all jingling with gold and silver and bronze, and our young lads marching behind them in their breeches and plaids with the pack-horses. They made a gay sight. We never thought they wouldn't come back – most of them, anyway. Mind you, I've seen sights that might have made you wish they hadn't. A face split open by an axe. An arm hacked half off at the elbow and turning green. I couldn't save them all. The Raven must have her share of blood. So the young girls would cling and cry when their sweethearts went. But the older women just twisted their aprons a bit, and sighed, and maybe hung a little something round their man's neck for luck. There's hard work to do without them, but, on the other hand, you can get a sound night's sleep, though it begins to get cold on your own when autumn's putting a frost on the grass.

Of course, it's different if it's a son.

So Gorlois was off again, and laughing as if he was glad to be away from his womenfolk and out of Cornwall. First off it had been Aurelius. He was the one that got his own back on that traitor, Vortigern. But Aurelius was dead, poisoned they say, and now it was his brother Uther that all the Britons were following. To tell you the truth, wise woman I may be, but I never bothered much about where our men were going to fight, or what it might mean for us down here if they won or got beaten. As far as I could see, it was all another kind of hunting and bloody sport to them. They said my own man fell in Kent, when his master was fighting him they called Hengist. I used to tie strong magic round his neck and a hard leather jerkin over his heart. But when his time came round it seems it wasn't enough. I wailed for him when they told me, and cried for him too, in private, in the straw. He was a good man, as husbands go. I've never married since. I didn't need to. I was well provided for, with my lady's babies to bring up, and as for the other, I know those that can bring the thunder in the blood better than any mortal man.

16

The night's my time. And by day my life was those three girls, and most of all Morgan.

I suppose that's the difference between us and Merlyn. Men off and doing, as if they could change the world by running about. Women staying at home, to hold things as they are. They move in straight lines, while we weave circles. What has been must come again, or so I thought. So I never spoke a spell against the Saxons. It wasn't them I feared.

All the same, I wasn't wise enough to stop our world from changing, though it wasn't a Saxon army that came marching over the Tamar in the end. Of course, I'd heard of Merlyn, even then. Who hadn't? That clever brat that was got by a devil on a nun. The weasel Vortigern, that sold our land for Saxon swords, he meant to make the boy a blood-offering for his stronghold that kept tumbling down. But Merlyn was too sharp for that. 'Dig under the walls and you'll find a pool.' So they did. 'Drain the pool and you'll find two stones.' So they did. 'Break open the stones and you'll find two dragons.' So they did. And the dragons fought, backwards and forwards, 'til the white one killed the red.

That's power that could make your hair turn white if you think about it too long. It's one thing for the wise, who have the far-sight, to see what's coming. But to make a king and a court and an army, plain men with not a morsel of magic between them, see it too, that's something few druids on earth could do. It drains the strength out of your heart even to imagine holding such a spell. But he was alive to prove he did it, and right-hand counsellor to Uther now. For all that, it was the red dragon he was fighting for.

Morgan darted away from me and ran up to her father's horse.

'Take me with you!' she begged him, as if this was just another hunt they were going on.

'Women don't go to war these days,' he laughed at her.

'Boudicca did! And Mab. And it was Scathach taught Cu Chulainn to be a warrior.'

'Times change. We're Romans now. We're not living in those old stories any more. Would you like to see your pretty mother slashed with battle scars?'

She made a face to show it wasn't her mother she cared for.

'When I'm grown, I'll fight for you. And if you die, I'll hunt the man who kills you, through the length of Britain. They'll make a new story about us that will be sung for a thousand years and more. How Morgan, daughter of Gorlois, avenged his honour.'

Oh, Morgan, Morgan. How could the little mite know how close to her the man that killed him would be?

The men were all laughing at her by now. Well, she was just a skinny, black-haired scrap of a child to shout so bold. Only her father wasn't laughing this time. It never did to speak to Gorlois of dying. He was the bravest man that ever I knew, and I don't doubt he was as foolhardy in battle as the rest of them. But if he fell, he had no son to follow him yet. And not for want of trying. So he glared at her with a face as black as his hair and swore at her to be quiet.

But she'll make good every word she said.

My lady rode a little way beside him to the high road, with the rest of us following along behind as if it was a May-time picnic. Dressed in a clover-coloured gown, she was, with a cloak of gold and black flowing out behind her. As brave and beautiful as the furze and heather that were blazing on the hills. She'd

18

taken mighty good care of the way she looked that day, to make sure he'd hold that sight of her in his mind 'til he came back again. But Morgan had spoilt it for her, talking of death.

So Ygerne bit her lip and glanced sideways many a time to see from Gorlois's face what kind of mood he might be in now. It was a narrow, tricky road she had to tread, being wife to him. He'd married her for the great beauty that she had, and still had after fifteen years, if you'll believe me. It's the soft Cornish air that kept her pretty cheeks as delicate as the wild roses and curled her hair when there was damp in the wind.

But she'd disappointed him three times now. Two girls she'd given him, and in pretty quick time too. So he'd still had hope the next one would be a boy. Then, nothing. Years they'd waited. Many's the time she'd come to me in tears and begged me to help her. As if I hadn't taught her everything a wife should know, and done a few things in private on my own account that should have quickened any barren cow this side of Bodmin. It worked at last, and mighty proud she was when her belly swelled for the third time. But she wasn't laughing when it came to the birthing. I've never heard a woman scream so. And Ygerne was no coward. I truly thought the child was killing her, and itself as well. But we got it out at last. And it was a girl. Morgan. You wouldn't think a thing so small could have done so much harm. Black as a raven she was, even then, with her hair already grown down to her waist while she was still in the womb.

I laid her beside her mother, who was as white as death. Ygerne asked one question, and I answered her. Then she turned away, and it must have cost her a mighty effort to move her bloody buttocks even that

19

far, after what she'd been through. She wouldn't look at Morgan. She wouldn't touch her. The wet-nurse had her from that moment. And then she was mine.

I didn't believe she'd ever have another child, and nor did she. But the two of us went to lengths I hadn't even dared up to then. I took her to places, women, yes, even men, that Gorlois might have killed her for if he'd known. The old faith is still alive, or you wouldn't be listening to me now. It's more than a bit of harmless medicine, a few charms in a bag, or a poke up the bum under the horse's skirt on May Day. She must have blood.

Ygerne had other ideas too. She went to the saint. To Nectan. As if that white-gowned hermit knew anything about woman's work. Lily-livered folk that call wine blood and bread flesh. Strong voices and soft hearts those Christians have. But it seems he knew a bit more than I gave him credit for, and she came away from his cell with a flea in her ear, duchess or no. She still went beside Gorlois on Sundays after that. She had to. She couldn't very well tell her husband what the saint had said, could she? But she'd a hard job keeping the anger out of her face every time she looked at Nectan. And there'd be times he'd keep his keen blue eyes on her when he preached about witchcraft. He tried looking at me, but I'd pull the hood round my face and stare at the ground or the sky 'til he'd finished ranting.

Oh, yes. I took their Eucharist with them. We all did. The gentry expected it. They say it was a Roman emperor first had the idea that a crucified man could win the world for them in battle. Well, the Romans have gone from Britain now. It seems their fighting Christ couldn't keep the North-gods out of Rome after all. And what have they left behind but monks and nuns without a sword between them? A shepherd's crook, and a bell, and a pen. That's all their weapons now. And maybe they're more dangerous like that. But the men can't see it. Gorlois still rode out to battle against the Saxons under the cross. But who his wife prayed to for his safety was another matter.

So she had to tread carefully. She was his treasure. The most beautiful thing he owned, as long she could keep her looks. The envy of every lord in Cornwall, and further than that, if they came west to see her. But every time he ploughed her now the seed never sprouted. She knew she'd failed him.

They'd reached the crossroads before she'd plucked up the courage to smile and put her white hand on his bridle, and lean across to kiss him.

'God-speed to your banners, my lord. Let Uther Pendragon know there is high blood beats in Cornwall. Come back to us swiftly with victory and with honour.'

And she hung a charm round his neck, like any good-wife.

She was a brave woman, and a beautiful one. She smiled at him and turned her head so that the cloak blew back from her shoulders and the sun shone behind her through her hair. She wanted to be sure he'd remember her so, and bring him hurrying back to her bed.

He grinned at her then. The wind was blowing over the hills and the white pebbles shone along the road, going east out of Cornwall. There was hard riding and brave adventure and maybe glory at the end of it. There was a light in his eyes that told me his heart was across the Tamar already. He gave her a great bear-hug that swung her clean out of the saddle.

'Never you fear, woman! By Beli and by the Bride of

Heaven, those Saxons shall never set foot in Cornwall to steal Gorlois's treasure!'

And he galloped away from her at full speed with never a thought for the lads that were striding out after him on foot.

He never noticed Morgan, holding up her arms to him for a last kiss.

Chapter Four

We were coming to the height of our own killing when
they rode back. Samain, I still call it. Fat sheep and
sleek cattle for the butcher. They drove them down
from the moors with the wool curling on the lambs'
backs and the shine of summer on the cows' red rumps.
We couldn't keep them all. Not with the grass turning
to sour mud in the winter and salt blowing in over us
from the sea or snow down on us from the hills. Winter,
we were all shut in, folk and beasts. There wasn't room
enough for them all in a narrow place. Or food, either.
So some must die and others live. Those we kept were
the ones that were the best for breeding.

It was a noisy, smelly old time, what with pigs' blood
running into barrels and cattle roaring at the knife.
And pilchards and mackerel hanging up to dry, all split
and skewered, with the seagulls screaming over the
buckets of guts.

We kept the feast the old way. We doused every fire
to show the summer was dead and gone. Then we
scared ourselves silly in the dark. To some like
Margawse it was just a game. But Elaine knew better.
We still had one of the Old Ones to kindle the new fire
on the top of the hill that would light every hearth for
another year. It was a good old blaze we made, and
then we broke the oatcake, and him that got the burnt
bit ran for his life. I daresay we were a bit freer that

year, with so many of the gentry away. We didn't mind
my lady, somehow. For all her fine clothes, she was not
so very different from us.

I can see Morgan's eyes as she crouched beside me,
watching it all. Wide and black as two pools in a bog.
She didn't need to be told what it was all about.

I could take my girls that night, and not be worried
they might come back sprouting. Samain's not like
May-time. We huddled close, but I don't need to tell you
it wasn't for want of that. We daren't look over our
shoulders into the dark for fear of what we might see. It
was the night of the dead.

May-time and Samain.

Sometimes I wonder if that's all life is. Breeding and
killing. The men to kill. The women to breed.

There's just a handful of us set apart, between the
right hand and the left. It's left to us to watch over the
heart of things, to keep the world from tearing itself in
two.

That lanky saint, Nectan, spent Samain a different
way from us. A lamp burning in his chapel all through
the night, and him flat on his face, praying for the souls
of the dead. And if you'd passed close enough by
Tintagel, you'd have heard the white nuns singing
psalms.

Gorlois had done his share of killing too. He and his
men came back slower, and looking well satisfied with
themselves. Like a cat that's eaten a hare and come
home to sleep it off.

When all the yelling and the kissing and the boasting
had died down, they slept all right. Sprawled out and
snoring, as though some fairy-woman had cast a glamour over them to stop their eyes and ears for a year.
Like a woman after childbirth, they were. All the
struggle and the pain and the fear behind them. They

24

were mighty pleased with what they'd done.

We heard that tale sung so many times I was heartily sick of it by Christmas. But Morgan could never have enough of listening. We were coming to the time of the year when we keep the fire blazing high on the hearth at supper-time and the white logs are still glowing at their ends by morning. It was good and warm to be crowded in the hall, with apples and nuts roasting on the hot stones and the ale going round more slowly as our heads began to nod. Morgan would curl up on the floor with her arms round her father's leg. And if the harper fell silent or the men ran out of bawdy stories, she'd dig her pointed chin into his knee and say, loud enough for them all to hear, 'Tell us, Father. Tell us the story of how you saved Britain at Mount Damen.'

And he'd give a great roar of laughter and toss the wine-cup back. But he never said no to the telling of that.

Blaen the harper would touch his fingers over the strings 'til they began to dance.

Jordan and Britael would leap to their feet on either side of Gorlois's chair. Like two tall schoolboys, they were, hardly more sensible than the day the three of them rode up to Ygerne's father's gate, for Gorlois to court his daughter. And it wasn't long before Jordan tumbled me in the orchard too, though nothing came of that. Well, they were fine warriors, both of them, that could make a man's blood beat faster and a woman blush and a boy's eyes burn bright with talk of battles. It was a fine tale they told.

'The Saxons came marching down from the north.'
'They'd sailed a great army across from the lowlands.'
'Fire flared where they passed.'

'They ruined towns and farms.'
'Octa, Hengist's son, and Eosa rode at their head.'
'Hateful helmets and armour spread over Britain's land.'
'They came down on York, proud city of the Romans.'
'It seemed that no one could save the people.'
'Uther summoned warriors out of all the west.'
'From Cambria and Cornwall and Rheged of the Lakes.'
'They marched across Britain, the Pendragon leading them.'
'The Cross of Christ was on their banners.'
'Gorlois rode at Uther's right hand.'
'A man cunning in battle, skilful and fearless.'
'The ranks of the Britons were few against the hosts of the Saxons.'
'Red blood flowed and brave men fell.'
'Terror came with the white dragon of the pagans.'
'By nightfall we were driven back to Mount Damen.'
'High on the hill we hid amongst rocks and hazel trees.'
'The Saxons dared not follow us in the dark.'
'Like foxes we hid in hollow holes in the earth.'
'Like owls we looked down upon the camp of our enemy.'
'Vast the hordes waiting for us on the plain.'
'They slept in their tents, certain of victory in the morning.'
'Uther summoned his chieftains in the darkness.'
'The noblest warriors of Britain met in counsel.'
'Gorlois of Cornwall spoke words of courage.'
'Gorlois, battle-hardened, gave daring counsel.'
'The chieftains sprang to their feet under the stars.'
'Hope returned to the heart of Uther Pendragon.'

Well, by this time, they were on their feet, swords
out. Real swords, with real edges on their blades, mind
you. Acting it out and going at it, hammer and tongs.
Morgan was ducking her head to keep out of the way of
them, and her eyes flashing with the glamour of it, like
any boy's.

They were creeping round the hall now, with long,
stealthy strides, and making sudden dashes to frighten
the women screaming into a corner if they could. Some
of them enjoyed that, I can tell you. And you can be sure
that Margawse was always just in front of those
swords, so that it brought the heart into my mouth. She
was a girl that loved danger, when it came from a man.

'The brave band of Britons crept down the hillside.'
'Night and mist were friends to the Pendragon.'
'In silence they drew near to the Saxon sentries.'
'The stars shook with the shouts of men alarmed.'
'Fear ran like fire through the tents of the invader.'
'The Morrigan washed a bloody shroud for them.'
'Men fell in darkness. Brother turned against
brother.'
'Octa, that mighty leader, was taken prisoner. Eosa
was captured.'
'Gorlois of Cornwall taught Uther the paths of
victory.'
'The Britons marched upon York with their banners
flying.'
'At the gates, in the sight of all the people, Uther
Pendragon spoke.'
'He gave chief honour to Gorlois, Duke of Cornwall.'

Morgan's little eyes were shining by then, and there
was colour in her white cheeks for once, almost as high
as her mother's.

'The night is a lucky time for Cornwall, then? A time to dare! We take our enemy in their sleep and win the game.'

I heard a little laugh behind my shoulder. It was Elaine.

'And who shall be our enemy in the night-time?'

I didn't take any notice of her, fool that I was.

I was looking at the three of them, towering over Morgan. Jordan, and Gorlois, and Britael. The firelight dancing in their faces. And them laughing and slapping each other on the back as they remembered how they'd won. I saw those three creeping up on a camp in the darkness. Their white teeth grinning in the mist before dawn. Taking their prize.

Gwennol Far-Sight, they call me. I should be ashamed.

Well, there'd been killing enough to last them 'til another summer. But as for the other . . .

I'd seen Gorlois look at his wife almost before he swung a leg down from his horse. She had a fair, round belly, after bearing three children, and she wore her gowns slender and her girdle pulled tight. But one look, one spark in his eye, and then he could see that was all it was. She hadn't kindled. I've seen that darkness in a man's face many a time, when my husband sat across the fire from me, looking at my barren belly.

Chapter Five

It was one day when the rain was sheeting down outside and we were all filling in the restless time before supper, cramped up together in the hall and everything stinking of damp.

'I suppose you're Uther Pendragon's best friend now,' laughed Morgan.

She was sitting between her father's thighs and pressing her head back against his kilt.

He jumped up pretty quick when she said that, and kicked her, though he never even noticed.

'Yes, by God and the Blessed Head of Bran! I'm the best friend he has.'

He was striding down the hall, striking his fist into his palm and shouting. But I saw Jordan looking at Britael, and the two of them lifted an eyebrow at each other. There's more to this yet, I thought to myself, for all they shout and swagger so loud about their great victory. What's come between Uther and Gorlois, then, if they were so thick as they say at the gates of York?

'But it was because of you he beat the Saxons, wasn't it?' Morgan was on her hands and knees like a black cat. 'You told Uther what to do. You took Octa and Eosa prisoner and freed the North from the hand of our enemies. It was all your doing, wasn't it? If you hadn't led them down the hillside in the dark, the

Saxons would have beaten you in the morning and
Uther wouldn't be alive and wearing the crown of all
the Britons now.'

She was mightily proud of her father then. And had
good reason to be, if the tales the bards sang were
only half true. He'd saved Uther's skin, and the rest
too, and turned the tide for Britain that year. They'd
gone rampaging up to the North after that, all the way
to the other side of the Wall. And goodness knows
what kind of chancy folk or devils they fought with
there. And everywhere they went the red dragon had
put the white to flight, or so they boasted.

Gorlois grinned. He couldn't help himself. Like
Ygerne, he wasn't as young as he used to be. But like
her, he didn't look as old as he was. Just a bit of grizzle
in his black beard, like an early frost. And his step
was spry and firm. For all the battles that he'd fought
he hadn't a limp or a scar to spoil his looks. He was a
handsome man, and a proud one too. And he liked to
be praised. Well, that's what they pay the bards for,
isn't it? And why he kept a hundred warriors in meat
and ale. 'Gorlois of Cornwall!' they cried when they
raised their drinking horns. 'Gorlois the Generous!'
'Gorlois the Gold-giver!' 'Gorlois who saved the North
from the sword of Octa!'

Well, that was well enough in Cornwall. They were
his liege men. But how would a shout like that sound
in Dyfed and Gwynedd and Rheged beyond the Wall,
and such outlandish places? How did the other chieftains like to hear Gorlois praised above the
Pendragon himself? Did Uther's bards sing the same
song at the king's court in London as Blaen did here? I
bet they didn't. It would have set the Pendragon's
teeth on edge, I reckon. No gold ring for the poet who
sang a song like that. It's a dangerous thing for any

30

nobleman to be praised above his king. It's shortened
many a man's life. What Uther wanted was a man
to give him good counsel, but then the sense to keep
out of the way and leave the fighting and the glory to
him.

But Gorlois couldn't see it. That's all his life had
ever been: blood and glory. A woman's blood or a
man's. He'd have victory on a bed or a battlefield.
Either way, he had to win. He wouldn't care that he
was riding into the jaws of death, with his breeches
on or off. Maybe he was right. Maybe it was better to
live and die the way he did, and not go creeping and
careful. He wasn't the man to save his skin and lose
his honour. Was he to change because Uther would
rather have a soul-friend that had no need of a
sword?

All the same, something was heavy on him. We
waited for him to come out with it. I know all our
heads were up and listening then. I've seen folk like
that at haymaking, when you can hear the wind rising
in the trees and you know the rain will be on you any
moment.

He turned at the door and came striding back and
thumped the table. I think he wished it was a man's
head.

'I *was* the king's friend!' he said. 'After Mount
Damen. He's young yet. He trusted me. I gave the
Saxons into the palm of his hand when they could
have split and skewered our skulls upon a stake next
morning.

'I rode into the north beside him. Gorlois, Duke of
Cornwall at Uther's right elbow. We crossed the
Wall.

'But there was a snake in the heather. Sliding and
slithering into the king's good graces. One of those

31

that slough their skins and shift their shapes.'

I sat forward pretty quick at that, and my heart was thumping faster, for he was getting pretty near to my own business here. I daren't meet his eye. I didn't know how much he knew, but he was sometimes shrewder than I took him for. Besides, I'd half guessed the name he meant. I hadn't thought that one would have come to the surface again so far north. But that was before I knew him. Like an otter, he was, that can swim miles under water, hidden from sight. You never know where he'll rise next. Or like summer lightning, he'll strike at you out of a clear blue sky without any warning.

'I say Vortigern should have killed him when he meant to, prophecy be damned! The fatherless boy! It's plain why his mother would tell a tale like that, isn't it? Either his father was the devil or she's no nun. He talked his way out of that, and he's been talking his way to fortune ever since. Worm-tongue! I'm a plain soldier. I say what needs to be said, and that's the end of it.

'I gave the king good counsel, and it worked. I only say what can be done tomorrow, and I'm proved right or wrong. I don't deal in dreams. I don't try to paint the future.'

All this while Morgan had been staring up at her father's face, like a puppy-dog at her master. But when he started to talk of dreams I saw her eyes wander to the door. The rain had stopped, as it often does just before sunset. The sky was flaming under great purple clouds, like the edge of a creeping fire in the heather that can't be smothered. And I remember all the beads of rain on the ends of the thatch began to glitter. You'd think they were rose-crystals on the trees of fairyland.

'Who is he?' she asked. 'Who is it who can dream a king's future for him?'

'That trickster,' he said, 'that came from no good man's bed. Merlyn, they call him. Emrys Merlyn. Like a jackdaw, he is. You never know where he's going to be popping up next, stealing what doesn't belong to him. And he's no warrior or even a licensed bard. Yet he struts beside the king now as proud as a prince.'

'And will the dreams he weaves for the king really come true?'

Her eyes were wide. But I didn't heed her. It was her father I was watching closely then, and I held my breath to hear him answer. Gorlois was no fool. Not when it came to wars and land and the big affairs of men. It was only the things closest under his nose he couldn't see. Emrys Merlyn was a big enough affair, in all conscience. But I hardly knew if Gorlois counted him as a man.

A chancy, crafty, dangerous creature, he must be.

It's a funny thing. I'd never met him, and never thought I ever would, then. But I'd heard enough. Even to think that name sent a quiver down my spine and set the blood throbbing between my legs. You'd think I was a young girl staring after a man who's never looked her way, but that her body's panting for. We're not so far away in Cornwall that tales don't come our way, and Gorlois could be generous to any passing poet. And lately the songs of Merlyn had begun to grow.

There's many a brave Briton lost his life because of that traitor Vortigern. He thought the Saxons were his friends and called the council of Britain to a peace conference. Fool, that saw the flower of our leaders hacked to death before his eyes. But the fatherless boy he wanted to sacrifice to save his stronghold was

cleverer than them. Merlyn slipped out of his grasp,
like a tadpole through your fingers. There were some
who swore he was a child of hell and others who
whispered he was heaven-sent. But what's heaven
and hell to the wise like us? Our power is in the earth
itself. In springs and stones and under the hollow
hills.

For a while after that Merlyn vanished from the
tales. He'd hopped out of sight, like a toad in the
grass. Some said afterwards he'd fled to the forests
beyond the Wall, others that he'd sat on a mountain
from which folk come back madmen or magicians.
But suddenly here he was again. And now it seems
our fairy toadling had turned into a prince, or one
that walked pretty close with them. Closer than Duke
Gorlois, by the sound of it. Our good lord wouldn't
forgive that in a hurry. He thought he was the one
who'd earned the right to have the Pendragon's
ear.

I was Gorlois's bondwoman, since the day he married Ygerne. And I've served him loyally, living and
dead, down to this hour. For his sake I ought to have
hated Merlyn then, even before what happened. Yet,
I don't know how it was, but every time I heard the
name of Emrys Merlyn spoken it was as though someone had put a finger on that spot between your legs
that I needn't tell you of. The one that sends a thrill
right through your body. Sometimes religion's like
that. I've known those that can kindle lightning in the
soul as hot as in the flesh. And sometimes both at
once. He was one of those.

So when Morgan asked if Merlyn would dream true
I knew the answer, even if Gorlois didn't. It scared
me. There are times when I can see the future. And
more often than not I wish I hadn't. I've seen a man

trapped under the sea, with the fish picking his face away. I've heard an unborn child walled up alive in its dead mother's womb. Weeping comes out of the future louder than laughing. But I haven't made what I see. I'm like Gorlois. I'll pluck and brew, and cast and chant, to bring about what we need for this year. I don't interfere any further than that. I wouldn't know how. But suppose a man or a woman fasted and suffered and prayed hard enough to sweat blood, and went out into the wild places and wrestled with devils 'til they were nearly driven mad. Wouldn't they come back with powers greater than a mortal witch? A man like that might change the course of the world.

Just for a moment I saw clear. There was something Merlyn wanted from us here in Cornwall. It was only for a heartbeat, but it nearly stopped my heart. But Gorlois was a plain man, a soldier.

'I told Uther we would beat Octa's host at Mount Damen, and come off that hill with our lives and honour. Then I took my good sword in my right hand and made certain that what I'd promised him came true. Well, this trickster Merlyn is a different sort of warrior. We'll see if he can hold his weapons as firm as I hold mine. But I don't doubt he'll use all his craftiness to turn what he says he can see into certainty.'

It was Morgan who dared to ask, 'What does Merlyn see for the future?'

But Gorlois just turned his back on her and yelled to the steward to ask if supper wasn't ready yet.

All this time Ygerne had been sewing. She bent her pretty head over the sweet honeysuckle she was embroidering, as though it all meant nothing to her. Swords and sorcery. What was that to Ygerne? The Duchess of Cornwall, safe in her hearth and her hall in Bossiney. She was far away from the glamour of kings

and enchanters. I could kick myself now, looking back.
I knew better than to believe that on one score, didn't
I? She had more ambitions of sorcery than her
husband dreamed of. I was as big a fool as him not to
have guessed she might have ambitions for the other
too.

Chapter Six

So we came to primrose time. A wet, old winter since Christmas it had been, too, with all the tracks out of the dun running like rivers, and my Lord Gorlois sulky because there'd hardly been one day in seven that was fit for hunting. And all of us coughing and shivering, and the wood too wet to give a good blaze. I feared for Morgan then. I never thought we would bring her through the winter. There was always that feeling on me when I looked at her, as though she was never surely with us.

I've lost many a night's sleep over that child. Aye, and it began right back before she was born. I held her mother's shoulders when she was doubled up with pain. We feared for the child even then. We never thought we would get her to the birthing. And when we did, it seemed as if my lady would die too, with the child still trapped between her legs. And when it was all over, and the blood and the mess cleared away, what had we got to show for it but a scrap of flesh and bone, like a half-picked chicken leg that my lord would have thrown to his hounds?

I sometimes wonder if it would have been better if she had died then. If all that pain and labour wasn't for worse than nothing. But I can't think it. Even if I'd known what was to come, I couldn't have taken the pillow and smothered her, though there are some who

37

say it would have been better if I had. It's funny how
it's the ones who give us the most trouble that we love
deepest. Take Elaine, now. She was as easy a child as
you could wish for. Hardly a tear or a frown we had
from her. You could tell she would make a fine mother
from the day she was old enough to play babies with
her dolls. But I danced at her wedding when she married a king and went to bear him fine sons, and I never
shed a tear. But Morgan. Even when they took her
away from me, before she was half-grown, I never
stopped thinking about her.

But now the wind had changed, and the sea settled
like cat-skin, and the sky was as blue as a girl's gown.
My lord was restless. He'd been cooped up too long in
Bossiney. The wind was drying the tracks and news
began to reach us again from outside Cornwall.

I remember that day. It was healing weather. A
little mist coming up off the streams at sunrise. Then
it was swallowed up in that bright blue sky, as if the
heavens themselves had opened their arms and lifted
all our chills and tears away from us. For the first
time you could feel the sunshine sinking into your
bones and doing you good. There are some of the wise
have a touch like that, when they lay their hands over
your heart.

Gorlois and the men were off at dawn hunting, and
Morgan with them. For once I was glad of it. Her legs
were growing longer, and mine were getting slower
with every year. Sometimes the child would sit for
hours, hardly moving. Then she'd be off, as quick as a
stream over a waterfall, and how was I to keep up
with her, or know what was in her head? Let her
father look to her for once, I thought.

Small hope of that. I waved to her when they rode
off, but she never turned her face to see. She was too

busy trying to keep her pony's head as close behind her father's horse as the men would let her. And him? He couldn't wait for the hounds to give tongue to gallop away at the head of them all. He was so hot to kill whatever might cross his path that I don't think there was a thought in his head about her.

It was always peaceful at Bossiney without the men. We all found some excuse to be out of doors, and outside the walls too, if we could find the chance. The sheep were crooning in the pasture, and the lambs beginning to come. In a few weeks it would be Maytime, and summer on the hills. The whole place was like a daisy-flower opening up its petals to the sun.

I busied myself about our sleeping-hut a bit quicker than usual. Elaine's corner wasn't much trouble. Neat and warm and soft as a dormouse's nest. Margawse was the one that made me work. Clothes flung everywhere as she'd rummaged through her chest, sorting out what to flaunt herself in this morning, and the bedclothes all over the floor as if she'd been snatched from her sleep by a gang of Irish pirates. I scolded enough, bending my stiff back to pick everything up, though there was no one around to hear me.

I'd no need to scold Morgan, and I could have wished I had. Her bed-place was straight and tidy as a nun's, or a soldier's. That sometimes made me want to cry. It didn't seem natural. I was not so silly as to think she did it for my sake, to save me work. It felt more like a warning, telling me to keep off. She didn't want even my hands on her things, prying and poking. Not Gwennol's hands, that had reached inside her mother, when the midwife didn't dare, and pulled her into the world.

When that was done, I took a girdle I was plaiting,

and sat outside on a bench where I could feel the sun
on my face. I looked about for Margawse, but I
couldn't see her. Yet I didn't go looking for her. Not
then. I was pretty easy in my mind that morning. With
most of the men off hunting, and only a handful of
slaves about the place, there was little she could get
up to. There was a ruddy-faced shepherd boy I'd
noticed her sidling off towards lately. But I'd taken
care to have a word in his ear and I'd frightened him
good and proper with a picture of what evil I'd put on
him if he laid a finger on her. I left him shaking so that
the poor lad couldn't have got his tool up if Arianrhod
herself had come tempting him.

But I'd got used to looking for a whisk of her gay
gown round some corner, and I couldn't see her. Or
Ygerne and Elaine. They could be in my lady's bower
across the way, but why would they sit cooped up
indoors on such a sweet morning? I tried to put the
thought out of my head, but it wouldn't let me rest.
Every time I looked across at Ygerne's half-open door,
it had a still, empty look about it. There wasn't a
flicker of movement or a woman's voice from inside.

Presently it got so I had to find out. I unknotted the
wools from my waist and went across to look. I didn't
need to push the door wide open to know the truth of
it. There was no one in the chamber. I went across to
the hall, though what would they be doing there at
that time of the morning, among all the sweeping and
scrubbing after last night's supper? Issey, the
steward, must have seen me staring round and asked
me what was the matter. But I didn't tell him. I had my
pride. He was a decent enough man, but I wasn't
going to have a hall full of slaves knowing my lady had
taken her two daughters off, without even a word to
their nurse about where they were gone. I didn't want

40

them thinking I was too old for my job.

But you can't hide much, living as close as we did. I was taking myself off across the yard, and thinking I was keeping my dignity, when Ewa came past, carrying a bucket of ashes. A cow-faced slave, she was, from up Devon way. She'd never liked me. She grinned at me now, black teeth and all.

'If it's my lady you're looking for, she's long gone. She and her woman Ruan took themselves off just after sunrise. Carrying baskets, to gather the new herbs, they said. She called young Lady Elaine to go with her, and Tual to follow behind to guard them. And then I saw the Lady Margawse go running after them. Funny you not knowing that.'

I could see now why she was smiling so slyly. All the women knew well enough what I was. Not the whole of it by a long way, of course, but enough to make them look up to me more than ever they'd have done if I'd been just those three girls' nurse. They feared me more than a little. And it didn't make them love me, though there's many had reason to be grateful to me, and some for their lives, and their children's. But my lady and her daughters had gone off this morning with their baskets, on what should have been my business before anyone else's. And if I didn't know it, then maybe it was more than Gwennol Far-Sight's legs that were getting stiff and old? Maybe I wasn't the powerful wise woman I used to be, I could see her thinking, plain as if she'd said it out loud.

'There's those that can gather weeds and others that know who to use them on,' I snapped back at her. And gave her a look that sent her hurrying off to the midden with the blood running out of her cheeks.

But it hurt me sorely. Maybe I was getting too soft and slow, drowsing there on the bench when others were busy, and not seeing what was going on under my nose.

I put a shawl round my shoulders and a basket over my arm. I had a good look round to make sure that Ewa wasn't spying and I was off, out of the gates, as fast as I could go.

When I was out of sight of the dun, I stopped to catch my breath. It was a fair, fine day. There were little leverets hopping about in the grass between the hawthorn bushes and red squirrels leaping and shaking gold from the hazel catkins. But I stopped myself smiling at them and shut my eyes. I listened, deep inside. They couldn't hide from me. When I knew where they were, I went into the coombe and up the side of the brook, towards Nectan's waterfall. I didn't need to get that far. Just once I stopped to get my bearings. Then I left the water and began to climb up the steep bank through the trees.

I caught sight of Tual first, sitting on a big mossy stone, with his cudgel on his knees. Then I saw Ruan and Margawse were curled up at his feet. He was telling them some tale from the old wars with the Irish pirates that made them laugh pretty loud and shameless.

He saw me before they did and broke off quick, and they jumped up as though they'd seen a spirit-woman at Samain. Ruan turned her head very sudden, and opened her mouth as if she was going to call out to her mistress. But she thought better of it and laughed at me instead.

It seemed it was a smiling sort of day wherever I went. The sun smiling so sweet and friendly. The faces smiling so sly and secret.

Margawse said, 'Have you come all this way looking for us, Gwennol? You shouldn't have worried.

42

Look, you're all out of breath. Mother said she knew what herbs you would want us to pick. Then she took Elaine, and told us not to follow for a while. It seems there's things I'm not old enough to know yet!' And she laughed, so I could have slapped her face.

'We're all right. We've got Tual to look after us.' And that made Ruan laugh as well.

I was too full to answer her. For once it wasn't Margawse I was worried about. Tual was a slave. He wouldn't touch her, though he could foul her thoughts with his stories. I climbed right past the three of them as if they hadn't been there. Ruan called out after me, but even she daren't try and stop me, though she was pretty thick with her mistress these days.

I found Ygerne and Elaine. They were where I had seen them all this time, under a sycamore tree that was making yellow patterns of sunshine on the floor. They must have heard Ruan shout. They were crouched like two startled hares, watching me coming. I didn't say anything. I stood over them with my hands on my hips and stared down at them. I named over the leaves in their baskets and pursed my lips. I knew there was more than that to it. Then I saw it, half hidden under the skirt of Ygerne's kirtle. They hadn't been sharp enough when they heard the warning. I bent to pick it up. A chain of flowers. A dainty thing. Any village maid might have made such a garland to hang round her lover's neck. Until you looked closer and saw what was woven into it. Well, I needn't tell you. They both had blood, and more, under their fingernails. They'd used hooked flowers of course. Those that catch and claw and bind. I held it under my lady's nose, so she had to back away. But still I didn't understand what it was she wanted.

'What's this, then? A spell of summoning? Your

man's not at the king's court on the other side of
Britain now. Do you need such a chain to bring him
back to you from a day's hunting?'

She smiled at me, sweeter than any of the others.

'Elaine's new in our ways. There are things she
needs to be taught. And after such a cruel winter the
forest is full of fallen trees and dangers. The wolves
are hungry. There's no harm in us wishing Gorlois's
safe return, is there?'

She never thought of Morgan.

I looked her squarely in the face 'til her eyes fell.

'There are charms for a man's safety. I've filled
bags with them by the hundred. And there are spells
of binding. Do you think I'm so old and witless I can't
tell the difference?'

She always had an answer. 'Summer is coming.
Don't you feel it today, Gwennol? Soon Uther
Pendragon will be at the wars again, and Gorlois with
him. Should I not try to bind him to me, while there is
time?'

I saw her put her hand over Elaine's to keep her
quiet. The daughter's face was as sweet and smiling
as her mother's. But her eyes looked scared. I made
up my mind I'd have it out of that girl before the day
was over.

It was noon before we got back to the dun, and by
then I didn't need to be told who that pair had been
summoning. There was a horseman in the yard
already.

Chapter Seven

By nightfall the whole dun was in an uproar. That messenger wouldn't tell his news 'til Gorlois came home. It seems this message was too important for women's ears, even Ygerne's. But we found out pretty quick he came from Uther Pendragon's court up in London. Well, you can imagine the wild stories that went flying round.

'Are they going back to war already? They must be, mustn't they?' says Margawse, gripping me by the wrist as though she'd like to break it.

'Tual says the Saxons have brought a huge army over from the Lowlands to rescue Octa and Eosa.' Elaine's eyes were so big, I didn't know if she was more frightened of the Saxons or of what she'd done.

'They've captured Glastonbury.'

'The Picts have crossed the Wall and they're pouring south.'

I hardly knew where to turn or who to believe. It was too far even for my seeing, and it sounded like fighting men's business, none of mine. Except when Ruan said that about the Isle of Glass. The womb of Britain. That shook me for a while. I've never been so far, though I could take you to other tors, true daughters to that one. But we all know of it, of course, through the Old Ones. And I could feel it then, like a cord that's not yet cut, as if I was a baby feeding on its mother's blood. I'd have known if they'd touched that.

I was watching Ygerne as close as I could through all that flying about and foolishness. She'd got Uther's messenger in the hall and had the fire built up, and she was giving him the best wine in a jewelled horn, just as if he'd been the king himself. And all the time her little white fingers were tap, tap, tapping on the table-top. It didn't do her any good. He knew his job better than to unbutton his lips at the first drink he downed. She had to wait, like the rest of us.

It was still early in the year, and the light was turning purple over the forest before the hunt came home. And then, of course, I had Morgan to wash and get to bed. The poor little mite was so weary she could scarcely hold her eyes open. Still, she half knew there was something going on. She stirred and struggled a bit as I picked her up. Then her head dropped on my shoulder and she let me carry her to our hut. I stripped the muddy clothes off her back and bathed her and salved her scratches. She was so limp and spiritless you'd think she'd been drugged for the Offering, and I don't mean any Christians' Eucharist, either. I chased that idea away pretty quick. I laid her down on her bed, and lifted the black hair away from her little face. She was asleep before I kissed her. A little baby thing she looked on her pillow. And the only still creature in the dun, or so it seemed that night.

I couldn't wait to be off and running across to the hall as fast as I could go. It irked me to be called a wise woman and now to be the last to know the news. I'd have to keep my mouth shut and my ears open, and make believe I knew more than I did. But I needn't have worried. Margawse came flying across the hall as soon as she saw me.

'Gwennol! You'll never guess the news! It's not the

Saxons. Just the opposite. King Uther Pendragon is going to wear his crown at a great feast in London. All the lords in every part of Britain who helped him to victory are summoned to his court on Easter Day. And their ladies with them. Think of it, Gwennol! Mother's going to London to meet the king!'

I looked across at Ygerne and nodded. So that was the way of it. She'd been a better pupil than I thought, this daughter who was not of my own blood. She'd got what she wanted, and hadn't even asked my help. Only Elaine's. I watched her now, still smiling over the Pendragon's messenger, like any good housewife with a guest. Well, good luck to her, I thought. It's dull enough for her here in Bossiney, out of the way of all the great happenings. We don't see many kings down here in Cornwall, except him who calls himself King of Dumnonia. Of course, I'd been up Exeter way once. His court was a bit grander than our Cornish rounds. They'd built it up with stone the old Romans had left. It must have been a fine city once, before the pillars started tumbling down and the trees grew up through the pavements. But his house wasn't much richer inside than we were used to. That was long before, when Ygerne was newly-married, a slip of a girl as bright and golden as a Lent lily. She turned men's heads wherever she went. Since then, I'd had her children at my knee and stayed at home when they rode off to their kin across the Tamar.

Gorlois was like a dog that's seen a hare. He was mad to go. Anything to be off and doing, meeting with other lords and ladies and playing the great man. I could see him now, his arm round Ygerne's shoulders and fondling her more than I'd seen him do for many a year, except at night when he was drunk and couldn't wait to have her in bed. I knew what he was thinking.

Uther could wear his golden crown, to show to all the
Britons. But Gorlois had his golden Ygerne, and the
king might hunt a long way to find a wife more beautiful than his. She'd be his jewel.

As for his men, there were hands on daggers before
they'd hardly started drinking. Gorlois couldn't take
a hundred warriors to the feast with him, but he'd
want an escort. The Duke of Cornwall's got to look
like a noble lord. He fancied himself as a great chieftain now, since that battle. Uther's general. A bigger
man, they said, than our king up in Devon. So some
could go and some must stay. And who would he
choose for the honour, and why? They might have
beaten the Saxons for the moment, but there'd be
more blood shed in our hall over that victory, long
after it was won.

If we thought we'd had excitement enough that evening, it was nothing to what the place was like next
morning. All of us were sent flying about, and
screaming at each other like birds at mating-time.
There were the finest clothes to be looked out and
made good, and the jewels and the armour, and the
horses to be seen to. And all the food for the journey.

And in the middle of it all, while I was stooping over
the well, I heard Elaine's voice behind me. Clear and
calm, she sounded, just as if she'd been expecting it.

'Gwennol, you must get out my finest garments as
well, and make them ready. I am to go to London with
Father and Mother to feast with the king.'

I turned round sudden, and she was smiling down
at me, with that same smile on her face she'd had in
the woods, only not so scared now. Like a cat that's
had the cream and knows you're too late to stop it.
That look gave me a queer kind of jolt. It's one thing
to whisper a maid and watch her grow into a wise

woman, as I had with Ygerne, in place of the daughter
I never had. But when your spirit-daughter whispers
her own, and the two of them go spell-speaking in
secret with never a word to you, you feel as though
the world has turned a bit too far. Your star's already
gone down into the dark under the earth.

Well, I could see what was in her mother's mind
straight away. It was plain to all of us. Elaine was a
woman now, with a bloom in her cheeks like the wild
rose. And what better chance could there be to marry
her off to one of the highest in the land? Though I did
think that feast might be a bit like the midsummer
horse-fair, with the men sizing up the fillies for breeding and beauty, and their wives knowing it wouldn't
be just their sons' pleasure those lords were thinking
of. There'd be some sharp bidding and bargaining. A
duke's daughter may be bought and sold, the same as
a slave. And Elaine was a beauty, or so they told me. I
guessed that when that feast was over she wouldn't
stay a maiden much longer, and a good price paid, for
those that reckon in farms and forts. But when she did
come home, and sooner than any of us had looked for,
she had a tale to tell that was stranger than any I
dreamed of then.

There are some that get what they want through
the old knowledge. But there's other ways too, for
those that haven't been spoken. We had reckoned
without Margawse. Well, I can't be keeping my eyes
on them every moment of the day. I had enough to do
with helping to get all my lord and lady's gowns
washed and mended and trimmed, and Elaine's too.
You'd have thought they were going to London for a
year, they wanted so much, and we'd be lucky if we
could find wagons enough to carry it all.

I heard screaming in the great hall. I put my head

inside, and there were Margawse and Elaine, fighting
on the floor like two cats. That was a fine to-do, with
all the house-slaves standing round and gaping. Some
of them were laughing their heads off and the rest
were scared out of their skins. But there wasn't one of
them that dared lay a hand on those young ladies.
Ladies? There was hair and spit and straw flying
about in the air and I could see pretty soon there'd be
blood too if I wasn't quick.

'Stop them!' I screamed.

Well, those slaves looked at me once, but they
wouldn't move. And I hadn't the strength to separate
them. Elaine's strong. She may look plump, but
there's muscle there under the fat. She'd got
Margawse's wrists in a grip and was forcing them
away from her face, and kneeing her at the same time
for all she was worth. Margawse's eyes were blazing
like a smith's forge. She knew well enough she had
weapons at her fingertips. But she was so wild she
hardly knew where she was hitting, or Elaine's pretty
face might have been in rags before then.

I doubled out of that door and yelled for help at the
top of my voice. Well, that brought the warriors that
were in earshot running. They must have thought the
Saxons had found their way to Cornwall at last. The
swords were out before they reached me. They soon
saw what was what, and that it wasn't fitting for
slaves to see what they had seen, in daytime, and not
even strong drink to blame it on. Though goodness
knows I've seen worse than that at a feast when a fine
lady's husband has been given a portion meaner than
she thinks he deserves. Anyway, it was Endoder, our
horsemaster, and Hedrek, Gorlois's huntsman, that
had the separating of them, as if they'd been a pair
of their own bitches. They'd put up their swords and

dropped the shields they'd grabbed when they saw it
wasn't men they had to deal with. But they'd have been
glad of them. They took a wound or two, before they
had those two under control. If they'd been boys, I
think the men would have ducked them in the horse-
pond, for all they were Gorlois's children. But they
daren't do that to his daughters, even then.

I was gasping as if I'd been in a fight myself.

'You wicked girl! What if you'd scratched your
sister now and spoiled her looks, just as she's going to
the king's court to find a husband?'

Margawse laughed in my face. I'd handed her the
weapon she wanted.

Well, she went straight to her parents, as though she
was the one who'd been wronged. I fancy my Lady
Ygerne must have heard what was passing. Her bower
was not so far from the hall, when all's said and done,
and she'd sharper ears than I had. But she wasn't
going to interfere, or daren't. But when Gorlois understood how they'd shamed each other, with their skirts
up round their bums for half the world to see, he was
for whipping the pair of them, never mind who had the
right or wrong of it. But Margawse put her hands on
her hips and said, 'I want to go to the crown-wearing.
And if you don't take me, I'll put such scratches on
Elaine's face that no one will marry her, now or ever.'

Well, they threw me out pretty quick, and the rest of
us besides. But half the dun heard them shouting at
each other. He was furious, for she made him look as if
he couldn't manage his own womenfolk. But he knew
she meant it. She'd got the upper hand of them all. They
could have threatened to banish her or whip her, but
she only needed a moment. They couldn't act quick
enough to be certain she wouldn't reach her sister
before they could stop her.

And besides . . . she might not be fully woman yet, as I knew. But I'd seen her stroking her breasts when I bathed her. It wouldn't be long now. And there were few that saw her that would have guessed she wasn't. She could make every head turn when she walked through a group of men, and she knew it. And it wasn't only heads she stirred, either. There'd be more than a few wet breeches. She couldn't be wed yet, but there'd be plenty would be willing to offer. So she got her way, and I'd more work than ever to do making ready for her, and less time to do it in too.

The moment they told me Margawse was going with them, I knew what would follow. *She* didn't fight her sisters or run to her mother. There was only ever one person who counted with Morgan.

She stood in front of her father, pale as ever I'd seen her, and deadly serious.

'Take me! You must take me with you. You have to,' she said, very low and clear, and looking hard into his eyes.

It twisted my guts to hear her. She was trying to make it sound like an order. But I could tell she was desperate. It was just as if she knew he was going to say no, but was driving herself on to do it just the same. She'd damn herself first in her own heart, but she wouldn't stop 'til she'd heard him do it to her with his own lips.

Well, of course, he did. How could they have taken her? A little runt like her, who didn't even look the eight years she was. They'd have laughed her out of court, and him with her, parading herself like her lady mother and her sisters. Margawse would get away with it, and brighten plenty of eyes into the bargain, but never Morgan. That was always the way of it. Her father tried to laugh his way out it, of course.

That great laugh, that men think will set the world to rights and make women love them again. He put his arms round her to swing and hug her the way she always wanted. But she slapped his face and wriggled out of his clutches. That didn't please his lordship. He was as quick to anger as she was. So they were not good friends when he left for London. But what could she have done if she'd gone with him? He was no more cruel to her than she was to herself.

She ran out of the door. It never crossed her mind to threaten Margawse's trick. She wasn't like that. If she'd wanted to strike her sisters, she'd have done it there and then, without any warning. No matter that it wouldn't have got her what she wanted. It would have been quick and sudden, while the fire was eating her heart. She wouldn't think to wait in the dark, plotting to get her own way. She had a boy's temper, not a woman's wiles. Not then.

Chapter Eight

I remember the day they left for London, with Morgan still torn between loving her father and hating him. We were all up before dawn and in such a commotion, you'd think the king was coming to us, and not the other way round. Elaine was the calmest. She was ordering the packing of her mother's things, and her own as well, and making a better job of it too, for my lady was as excited as any girl. Margawse was nowhere to be seen, and goodness knows what she might be up to behind the armoury, but she was too big for me and I was too old to go chasing after her, and so I'd told her mother many a time.

Down in the stables they were grooming the horses 'til you could see your face in their backsides, as if they wouldn't be spattered with mud and sweat by the time they crossed the first ford. I found Morgan down there talking to her father's horse. She was twisting her fingers in his mane as though she wished she could turn into a fly and hide herself away there when he rode off. We must have been the only two in the dun standing still, and not dashing about with our faces all red and bothered. And then Issey, the steward, came running, like a man demented, and calling out that my lady had ordered sweet-meats to be baked for the journey and the honey was all gone, and there wasn't another spare pair of legs to go to the bee-woman and get more, and would I fetch some for the cooks? I burst out laughing in his face. The sun was over the trees already. This was no time to start baking cakes. They should have been on the road and over the hill long before this, and so I told him. But he was as crazed as the rest of them.

'Use your eyes, woman! It will be hours yet before they're ready. Hurry now, before they think of something else to trouble us with.'

Then Gorlois's horse reared up at the shouting and swung Morgan off her feet. She screamed, and dropped down to the ground almost under his hooves. And as bad luck would have it, up came Lord Gorlois behind me, yelling, 'Get that child away from here, you old fool, before she gets trampled to death.'

Well, I can tell when I'm not wanted. I grabbed Morgan with one hand and the empty crock Issey was holding out in the other and took them both off.

I had trouble with Morgan. She tried to snatch her hand away from mine and run back, though her father had marched off out of sight again.

'No, Gwennol! I'm not going! You can't make me. They're going to leave without me and I won't even have said good-bye to him.'

'You great fool,' I told her, sounding like Issey himself. 'Look at them all, running about like a troupe of mummers at Christmas-time. It'll be noon before they're on their way, and they won't leave without your mother's sweet-cakes by the sound of it.'

'They will! They will! You know what she's like. She'll forget she even ordered them. I *won't* go.'

She had the stronger will, but I had more weight. I was fairly dragging her towards the gate, and she had marks on her wrist afterwards to show for it. But I'd lost patience with them all. If I was to be ordered about like a house-slave, I'd do my share of ordering too. Still, I had to calm her, or she'd be darting back like a swift the moment I let go of her.

'Now then, you can see they haven't harnessed the horses yet. And it isn't so far to walk to the bee-woman's. You'll have them in sight when we're on the downs. If they look like leaving, you'll see it soon enough to run and catch them.'

'Are you sure, Gwennol? Are you really, really sure?'

'And your father wouldn't leave without a kiss from you, would he, now?'

She looked at me then, with eyes so dark it was like peering into the night. They told me nothing. But I think it was me saying that that decided her. She was putting him to the test. She must have known he'd fail her.

She darted off ahead of me out of the gate. I picked up my skirts and hurried after her. But I soon slowed down. I couldn't walk very fast, even then. It was quiet up on the cliffs. Just a bit of a breeze in the grass and the gulls flashing overhead, and the little spring flowers beginning to come out. It would have done me good to have sat down and rested in the sunshine. Across the bay we could see the white huts of the nunnery on Tintagel Head. Very still and quiet they looked, like birds nesting on a cliff, hatching their young.

It was a queer feeling. You'd have thought we should have been bitter enemies, me and those Christians. That hoarse-voiced beanpole, Nectan, up the coombe, ranting at us for our sins on Sunday. Those clear-faced nuns, busy as bees, growing queens to stock new hives all over Cornwall. And so we were, when we were each about our own business. I can still feel it like a blow to the stomach – the day they overturned the Stone Man of Trigg. I looked for the heavens to open and shiver their cross to splinters, and the unholy hands that raised it. But the gods must have hid their faces from us that day. Next year we watched those white-robed women marching over the bridge to Tintagel Island, with their cross held up in front of them, singing psalms. Yes, and we did more than watch, some of us. I was a young woman then, drawn up with the rest of the wise on the cliffs opposite, hurling slates and screaming curses on them.

The stones didn't reach them, and the wind took our curses away and turned them back on us, it seemed. Gorlois saw to that. He thought himself a proper Roman then, giving those Christian women the land. Never mind that it had been sacred to us long before their time. He wouldn't let us near enough to harm the nuns. Not with our hands, anyway. There's other means. The Romans have gone, and we'll see who lasts longest now, the Latin psalm-singers or us.

Well, they could drive us from the high places under the sky. But most of them didn't know what went on still, in the dark places you all know of. Though there were some even among the nuns that kept the old faith in secret. That made me laugh. And Gorlois never guessed where his own wife went by night when the month came round again. Most of our gods are like any war-lords. They can be beaten. But the Mothers will go on giving birth. You can't stop them.

Gorlois's people followed him to Nectan's chapel, willing or not. And there were some of the gentry who sent their daughters to the nuns to school, to learn to read and write and weave a pretty embroidery. But we weren't idle, either, though we had to be careful and secret the way we went about it.

58

So you'd think I'd have hated those nuns, looking across at the place that was once ours. But I couldn't somehow. We were like a pair of wrestlers, sizing each other up. The men who ruled us couldn't see what was going on under their noses. But those women did. Not the whole of it, of course, but enough to respect us. We understood each other's ways. And sometimes I envied them, never mind their cold, narrow beds and their meek rules. They were on the winning side now. You could see by the light in their faces.

But the wise women know how to wait.

That morning I could have sat and looked at Tintagel for a long time, and those little white-robed figures going peacefully to and fro. It was so different from the folly we'd left behind us. But Morgan couldn't wait. She was as restless as a butterfly, flitting from one side of the path to the other. She kept getting further ahead and calling back to me to hurry. All the same, I could see she was glad to be out of doors again and feel the wind fresh on her face. I know I was. I couldn't even mind that it was blowing Morgan's hair all any old how, and I'd be half the day combing out the tangles, if I could keep her still enough. It was enough for me to see her happy for a moment and safely through another winter, though there wasn't a drop of colour in her cheeks, just the tip of her nose red with the wind.

She'd found flowers now, hiding in the moss under the stones, and she was picking a bunch of them for her father. Primroses, mostly, and a few violets. But she couldn't make them into a dainty nosegay as Elaine would have done. She snatched at them too quickly, so that some of them broke off short and others she pulled up by their poor bruised roots. It

was all pretty spring above her fist, but underneath
you could see the torn stems hanging down.

She was chattering away, as busy as a starling.

'When we get the honey, I'm going to make cakes
for Father too. Some he can have for the journey. But
I'll make special ones, Easter cakes, that he can give
to the king. He'd like that, wouldn't he? The king
would be pleased with Father if he gave him Easter
cakes, wouldn't he, Gwennol?'

'That's as may be. As like as not you'd run off and
forget about them, 'til they were burnt. The king
wouldn't thank your father for offering him a plate of
charcoal, would he?'

'I wouldn't! I wouldn't! They'll be the best cakes in
the world. And the king will send for the maiden who
baked them and offer her his hand in marriage. And I
shall be the greatest queen in the land. And when
Uther Pendragon is killed in battle, they will bring his
body back to me and I shall raise his sword and lead
his warriors to victory over the Saxons. And all the
people will shout, "Long live Queen Morgan, leader
of the Britons!" '

'Get along with you! You couldn't lift King Uther's
scabbard, let alone his sword. And if you dance too
near the edge of that cliff, you'll end up the seal-king's
bride, and a kingdom under the sea.'

Little we guessed then who Uther Pendragon's
bride would be within the year.

I was all for staying and chatting at the bee-woman's
cottage on Barras Nose. If I was to be treated like a
kitchen servant and shouted out of the way, I'd get my
own back on them by having a morning's gossip where
no one could see me. And the steward could whistle
for his honey. But before long Morgan began to tug at
my skirt. She was in a hurry to go, and full of the

presents she'd planned for her father, the little
flowers and the Easter cakes. My heart softened, for I
couldn't ever say no to her, though I made sure to
scold her for the fidget that she was.

All the same, I couldn't hurry back as fast as she'd
have liked me to, with the great crock on my shoulder
full of good thick honey now. We came over the cliffs,
and the flashing and movement from Bossiney was
like a fairground in front of us. Then we dropped into
the track that led up beside the stream away from the
sea and lost sight of the dun for a while.

It was a hollow way, and soft underfoot. Above our
heads the twigs of the hawthorn were bare yet. But
the Lent lilies stood as brave as golden war-trumpets.
It was very still and quíet, just as if we had stepped
into another time and another world. Down there
between the hedgebanks we lost the noise of the dun.
Morgan looked at me, and I saw the fear in her face.
She started to run.

We came out of the hollow road into the sunshine
before the gate. And it was a different sight now. The
horses were saddled and drawn up in lines, and the
slaves holding the pack mules' heads. Even before
they saw us, my lord was lifting Lady Ygerne into her
chariot. Margawse and Elaine were already sitting
up in theirs and smiling. Morgan stopped short with a
shudder, like a boat that's struck a rock. She dropped
her poor little flowers in the mud. Then she dashed
forward through the warriors and flung herself on
her father as he settled himself in the saddle. I was
left too far behind to hear what she cried at him. Not
that I needed to. She hadn't learned then how to trick
and act and smile falsely at men. I didn't need to come
within sling-shot of her to know what she would be
saying. Every line of her body and every twist of her

hands was shouting to high heaven. She had her fingers knotted in her father's cloak and her black hair was trailing down his horse's flanks like dried blood. But he flung his arms open and laughed at her, with his teeth white in his beard. Then he tossed her in the air and set her over his horse's neck. By the time I caught up with her, she was hugging and kissing him, though I could tell that underneath she was still angry to think that he might have ridden away without her, while she was still on the downs picking primroses for him.

You couldn't have told her, but it was her own faults in him that made her angry. She always did what she wanted. And when did she ever stop to think of the hurt she was doing to other people? Afterwards she'd give you a laugh and a kiss to make it all right. And where did she get that from but her own father, laughing at the world through his black beard?

Lord Gorlois handed her back to me.

'Bring me a present,' she cried. 'Something splendid from the king's court.'

'What shall it be? A golden goblet, studded with jewels? A cloak trimmed with fur? A wolfhound's puppy?'

'A sword! A magic sword that will kill every enemy!'

He laughed at that, and trotted away from us through the gateway. A fine, proud sight, with his warriors and ladies behind him.

Morgan looked up at me when they had gone past seeing her waving.

'I didn't give him the flowers. He didn't deserve them. He was going away without saying good-bye to me.'

She gathered up the flowers then, what was left of them, for they'd been trampled into the mud 'til they were pulped and broken. She should have left them there. But she could never let a wound alone. She always had to be testing it to see how much it could hurt. She laid those poor, battered stems across her hand and tried to straighten what petals there were left. I watched her little fingers, stroking and smoothing, as if even then she thought she could heal them. And I wondered, not for the first time either, if perhaps she shouldn't be whispered too, young though she was. No one that knew such things could doubt there was power in the child that she didn't know herself yet. It scared me sometimes. And if she knew the charms of mending she might be a great healer one day, as great as any I'd known.

But all of a sudden I shivered. I cut off the thought short, like the sun going behind a cloud. You can't build walls round a power like that. It goes where the wise woman wills. Left or right. To heal or to harm. I loved the little maid dearly, but I wouldn't trust her with knowledge like that.

So I fell to scolding anyone who was left to listen.

'Yes, and there's me with my arms nearly dropping off, carrying this great crock of honey. And what for, I'd like to know? A slave might just as well have fetched it tomorrow, for all the use it's been. It's not my place to go fetching and carrying like a mule. But your father's like a little boy. He's that excited to be going to see the king, he can't wait. And my lady's not much better, though I don't blame her for that. We see little enough of fine courts and palaces here, and she's beautiful enough to be a queen.'

Young Keby, the stable boy, was coming back from the gate. His cheeks turned red when he saw me and it crossed my mind that it might have had more than a little to do with Margawse disappearing that morning.

63

And maybe that was why he was in such a hurry to turn my thoughts another way.

He burst out laughing. 'Our lord's a lucky man, and he wants the king to know it. But if I had a wife with my lady's breasts, I'd be leaving her at home when I went to the Pendragon's court. I bet she's still good for a tumble in the straw, even if she has got two tall daughters and the little one. And from the tales our lads brought back last year about King Uther, he's not the man to keep his weapon under his cloak when there are pretty women about.'

'Shame on you, Keby Eval's son! We're not all as free with our hands as some I could tell of. That's no way to be speaking of the High King of Britain. My lady's a good woman, and true to her lord, and has been these fifteen years.'

'Don't shout at me. I didn't make the tales. And it's not my hands we're talking about, is it? I'm not the keeper of the High King's weapon. It wasn't me Gorlois swore his oath to, to give the Pendragon whatever service he asked for. You think of that, Gwennol Far-Sight.'

'My lord's a proud man who can take care of his own. And if you want to keep a whole tongue in your head, you'll keep your dirty thoughts to yourself.'

He looked round that empty yard with his insolent grin. There was only me and Morgan.

'Who's left to hear us now but you and me, Gwennol? And don't tell me you hadn't heard the Pendragon's put more than Saxons on their backs all over Britain. I'm only saying what half of Cornwall knows already.'

'Then Cornish folk can know from me that my lady's a pure wife, and always has been. And she's too wise to be having her head turned by a gold crown at her age.'

I don't know why, but I was trembling with anger so that I could hardly hold that stupid crock of honey in my arms. Time I got rid of it, and gave Issey a piece of my mind for putting me to all that trouble for nothing. It wasn't my place to fetch and carry. I looked round for Morgan. She shouldn't have been listening to such talk. But the wind had blown the tangles over her face and I didn't think she'd heard us. I should have known better.

Chapter Nine

It was a sweet spring, that year – with clouds like young lambs chasing across the sky, and the sea so quiet you could hardly believe how it had been tearing at the cliffs like a pack of wolves all winter. I've often wondered what it must be like to live inland and not to hear the come and go of the waves like blood in the ear.

Our coast looks north, and there's many a tumble of black rock that never sees the sun. But below Bossiney there's one sweet stretch of golden sand when the tide is down. You can sit there in the sun in the middle of the day and watch the green water washing in past the Sisters and a boat or two bobbing out at sea. There's tall old cliffs on either side. From there I couldn't see that stone cross on Tintagel Head, let alone what lay beneath it. When I look back, those are the days it doesn't hurt me to remember, when there was no one to trouble me but Morgan, and I didn't need to be looking up every moment at a warning of what was going to take my baby away.

It was an easy time for us, with our chieftain and his lady away at the court of King Uther Pendragon. And if I was resting my old bones in a bit of sunshine on the beach, mending an old gown for Elaine, who was to worry if Morgan was sometimes out of sight? I was feeling my rheumatism even then, and what would a stiff old body like me be doing scrambling

67

over the rocks of the sea-shore after an eight-year-old that was as nimble as a goat? If it had been Elaine, now, I'd have been worried sick that she'd slip and drown herself in the sea. But not Morgan. She was as sure-footed as a cat. Her sort don't fall. I scolded her often, mind you, but I knew she'd come to no harm. The sea was her playmate.

'Gwennol!' she said, and I nearly fell off the rock with fright, for I hadn't seen her in the shadow of the cliff behind me. She trumpeted with laughter and set me straight again and picked up my sewing from the sand. Then she squatted down in front of me and tipped up her sharp little face.

'Will they come here?' she said. 'My father and the king? If they're out hunting and it starts to get dark, would they ride this way and stay in our dun?'

'Goodness me, my lover! The gods forbid!' I said, and I crossed my fingers for good measure. 'They're miles and miles away. Across the Tamar and a lot further than that. A week's hard riding, or so I've heard tell. And a good thing too, the state we're in. The larder's almost empty and there's hardly a thing growing in the gardens yet but kale. How would we be feasting a king at the back end of winter, with not even a day's notice to brew and bake?'

'But they'd bring meat for the feast with them, wouldn't they? A great stag over the horse's back. Or a boar with savage tusks, and their spears red with its blood.'

'And what about your dear mother? Would you have her galloping half across Britain at her age?'

'I wasn't thinking about Mother.'

'I don't need telling that. You're too fond of hankering to run after the men, my handsome. But it's a woman's world you'll have to live in, so you'd better

68

make up your mind to it. I've enough trouble with your sister Margawse that hasn't eyes for anything that doesn't walk in breeches. We'd all sleep a lot sounder in our beds if that one was at school in the nunnery on Tintagel.'

'I'm not like her. Margawse doesn't want to *be* a man.'

She spoke true enough there. To tell you the truth, it wasn't just idleness that kept me in the dun most of the year. Elaine was as happy as a bird to borrow her mother's power over the hall and the kitchen, and see things were well-set and proper. It was Margawse I worried about. I could never see her disappear round some corner or into a dark doorway but I wondered who might be waiting for her there. She'd no pride. Only a red hunger that wouldn't be satisfied. As soon as she was a woman she ought to be married. I thought of May-Eve that was coming. If I could take her with me then . . . That was what she needed. There is a right season for everything. And those that open their blood-hole to the Mother's Son can sleep more easily in their beds on other nights. It wasn't as if she would be the first of her folk to travel that road, for all Ygerne's family were nobles and called themselves Christians now.

Elaine was still a maid. I'd taken good care of that, even after she was spoken. But her mother was a different story. Many's the time she's been into the Mother's Hole with me. She put on a mask and hood, and I blacked her face below so that no one would guess who she was. There's loose tongues among the wise, let me warn you, the same as other women. But there were some that had to know. Well, we have our own lords and ladies by night, as they have theirs by day.

Gorlois never knew the half of it. I told him there were women's times when he must keep out of her chamber. And what I threatened would happen to his parts if he didn't was enough to make any man sweat. He'd curse and shout if his blood was up that night, but he feared me too much to cross her threshold.

So we wrapped a mist round his eyes, the two of us. He may have known there were times and places I had to go where it would have been death for a man to follow me. But I swear he never guessed his own wife went with me. The gatekeeper knew better than to peer under the hoods that went past him. And she wasn't going to tell him. What we do in the Mothers' name we don't call adultery.

There was only one thing that chilled me – if that stringy Nectan should ever make a proper Christian out of Gorlois and tell him our threats were nothing but moonshine compared to his power. Oh, don't mistake me. My power is real enough. I can feel it sometimes, coming up through the soles of my feet out of the good earth. It runs out through my hands into things I touch, like blood from an open cut. But there's one thing can dry it up. A Christian unbeliever. Lucky for me, he never knew that 'til the day he died. And luckier for his sweet lady's life.

But Morgan was not like her sisters, or her mother. There was a proud spirit in every inch of her. You'd be cutting off pride with every snippet of her finger-nails that curled on the fire. You could see it even in the way she slept, so still and stiff under the furs, while Elaine snored so peaceful and Margawse tossed about. There was always that pride. She would risk anything to get what she wanted, that child. But it wasn't what Margawse wanted. What Morgan dreamed of was to be a queen – or better still, a king.

She sat quiet, looking out to sea. There was a mist starting to rise from the woods in the coombe behind us and the sun was going down over the clifftop for another day. She could sit very still indeed, when she wanted to. I looked down to see what she had been making in the sand. I gave a great start and then hoped she hadn't noticed.

It frightened me. I'd never taught her. But it was there in front of me, or almost. She hadn't the pretty flowers her mother had used. She'd taken living things of the sea, or things that had been living. Empty shells, limpets mostly, and strands of cold wet seaweed, with holdfasts like fingers. But the pattern was the same. It only wanted blood.

'What's that you're doing there?' I asked.

'*You* know! Making a spell,' she said, jumping up with that wicked laugh and hugging me. 'To bring him home to me.'

I kicked that circle into little pieces. I didn't know why it was I had to keep that knowledge from Morgan. I'd never worried when Elaine was whispered. But there was a warning shouting inside me as if the tide was rising. And so it was. The sun had gone from our cove and there was a damp chill in the air. I grabbed her hand and hurried her home.

At dusk they shut the gate of the dun, and though we had nothing but cheese and beer on the table we were sitting late taking our ease when the dogs set up an almighty racket in the yard. Keby went running to the doorway and shouted out. 'Bran's balls, it's my lord and lady! And just look at the horses! You can hardly see them for dust and sweat. They've been ridden fit to break their hearts!'

Well, we were hard on his heels. And what a sight met us. The wild eyes of the horses rolling in the

71

lantern light like night-mares. There were riders leaping down off their horses and shadows of cloaks swooping about like great bats. There were those that shrieked as though they thought the Black Hunt had come to take us. But they were human, all right, and I don't know which of us was more frightened. Gorlois's bodyguards had their swords half-drawn, as if they expected to be attacked at any moment.

We women flew about like hens when a fox gets in among them. And squawking just as loud. The beds weren't aired, and there wasn't a loaf of fresh bread in the place, or a mouthful of stew in the cauldron. And some were dashing to change the rushes on the floor of my lady's chamber, where the puppies had got in and fouled it, and it hadn't seemed worth the trouble of changing them 'til we knew she was coming home. And now, when I look back at it, I can see we had fouler things than that to worry about.

I was running to and fro like a madwoman, not knowing what to do first. The chariot was empty when I got to it, and the furs all tumbled in the mud. I couldn't find my lady and the girls in the dark and for a terrible time I thought they had been killed or taken by the Saxons. And then I caught up with my lady stumbling towards the hall doorway fit to drop, with Elaine and Margawse holding her by the arms on either side of her.

As soon as I saw their faces, I knew that ours were nothing but children's troubles, slaves' troubles, beside what had happened to them. My Lady Ygerne was weeping and trembling something terrible. Yet for all that, her eyes were bright and you could see she was excited. It struck me suddenly that she was not as much like our little Elaine as I'd been thinking lately. There was something of Margawse in her still, even if she was twice her age. And it's not to be wondered at, for Morgan and Margawse were her blood too.

I didn't like the look of Lord Gorlois. He was angry but he was afraid, too. And that's not a thing I'd ever thought I'd see in him. He was as brave a warrior as you'd find anywhere, our Duke of Cornwall. He couldn't keep still and he had to be shouting and giving orders, though I don't suppose he knew what he was doing half the time. He just had to be on the move. He ordered the gates to be barred again and all the weapons in the dun sharpened and a strong guard to watch through the night. So we all looked at each other, but nobody dared to ask what was the matter.

I caught a glimpse of Morgan's white face as she ran from her bed towards her father. I called out to her, but she wouldn't listen. I could see he had no time for her, but she followed along behind him like a puppy-dog, waiting for him to notice her. I let her go. I had my hands full enough as it was. We took my lady round the waist and helped her to her own bower. She fell to weeping on my shoulder and she was all fluttering and trembling, like a woman when a man strokes her flesh and takes his time about going further. Elaine and Margawse came crowding after us into the bed-chamber. Elaine looked fairly shocked, but Margawse was dying to tell us all about it.

We set her on the bed and shook the cloak from her shoulders. All spattered with mud, it was. I set to brushing her hair, thinking that would calm her. But when we asked her what was the matter, she threw back her head and laughed, and then frightened us more by laughing and weeping at the same time. So Elaine ran to the kitchen for a beaker of hot wine and herbs. When we had quietened her down they told us everything.

Chapter Ten

Well, you must know by now what happened as well as I do. The bards have sung that lay the length and breadth of Britain. But what was strange was the different ways those three told it.

Margawse was gabbling away as if she couldn't get the words out fast enough. Her red hair was all tumbled over her shoulders and her eyes sparkling like a cat's. I'd seen her wild before, but never as excited as that. You'd think her gown would have split, her breasts were heaving up and down that fast.

'We've been in Fairyland, Gwennol! Such a city! I thought it couldn't be real. White statues on pillars, as if living people had been turned to marble. And such floors in his palace. They'd think shame to put rushes over them. They had pictures in little coloured stones. Can you imagine that, Gwennol? Pictures even on the *floor*! And as warm as summer. You could dance in your bare feet and it was as though the sun had been beating on the tiles, although it was night, in April, inside stone walls.'

Well, there was more of such nonsense. Baths steaming like boiling lakes. Couches of marble. Halls big as our grove in the forest, all under a great tiled roof. Whole streets of such palaces, she said, and the streets themselves paved with giant stones. Temples and churches to foreign gods and goddesses. Market squares. No wooden walls and thatch, you understand, but all made of great blocks of stone, if I was to believe her. Well, I saw Exeter years ago, and that was grand enough for me. But that was a hovel compared to London, if I was to believe her. You couldn't imagine such a thing, could you? I thought her head was turned and her wits were wandering.

Elaine was the one I could get most sense out of, though she was more scared than any of them, poor soul.

'Such crowds of people there were, Gwennol! And I don't just mean common folk, though the streets were thick with them staring at us. But fine lords and ladies from every part of Britain. I didn't think the world could have held so many. And the clothes and the jewels! We were like brown hedgehogs, all covered in dust and mud. But they took us into fine rooms and oh, Gwennol, they had hot baths as big as horseponds, and they washed our hair and oiled our bodies with scent, and we put on our second finest clothes, for we must leave the best ones 'til the grand feast of the crown-wearing. And then they led us to the great hall for supper and I thought that everyone would titter at us for country bumpkins.'

'The very idea!' I scolded. 'You two young ladies are pretty enough for princesses, and so I've heard say many a time, and you've gowns good enough for any duchess.'

'But they *didn't* laugh, Gwennol. All the heads were turning when we came in. I'm sure I was blushing like a gorse-fire. You know how it is when you feel everyone's looking at you. And they all seemed to have Roman names, like Lucius and Eusebia. And some of them called me Helena!'

Margawse couldn't hold herself in any longer. 'The king, Elaine! Tell her about the king.'

My heart seemed to jump a beat, and then took to hammering like a galloping horse. For what could she mean but that the king himself had looked at them, and which of my two young ladies would it be he'd set his fancy on? And then I remembered what young Keby had said and I turned cold again. It was true it wasn't the first time I'd heard that said about Uther Pendragon. I thought how a king can do pretty much as he pleases, and it's a bold father would say no to him, though it is his own daughters the king would have the maidenhead of. But when all was said and done, he surely wouldn't be ungrateful. A king's a king, and there would be few noblemen who could refuse to wed her for a cause like that, maiden or no maiden, and he'd know there'd likely be jewels and favours to follow for her and hers.

And it crossed my mind just then to hope it might have been Margawse he'd set his fancy on, child though she was, though you'd never have guessed it. For it would be common knowledge if the king took her, and none could shame her after that or know what she might or might not have got up to behind the armoury already. And I'd a shrewd idea the king wouldn't tell, whatever he found out about her, for he'd shame himself to let it be known he was not the first.

But which of those two was it, in truth's name?

'Be quiet, Margawse,' says Elaine. 'I'm getting to that. All in good time.'

'Tell her about the goblet. How the king sent it from the high table.'

Margawse's eyes were shining like two jewels in a goblet themselves, so I made sure now it must be her.

'*Well*,' says Elaine, getting cross because she wouldn't be hurried, 'we were all led to our places at the supper tables. And I could see Father was angry because he thought we should have been on the king's table.'

'And he was saying how he'd fought last year for Uther Pendragon against the Saxons in Elmet, and how he saved York for the Britons. And he was shouting it out loud enough for the king to hear, and people were beginning to look at us for more than our fair faces.'

'I started to be afraid then,' Elaine confessed. 'And I'd been so enjoying it 'til then. It was like a fairy-tale. Everyone treating us as though we'd always been princesses but never known it. And then I got frightened because of Father shouting, and I thought perhaps we couldn't have been princesses or we would have been up higher, as Father said. And maybe those lords and ladies always treated each other like royalty and there was nothing special in the way they looked at us.'

'But there *was*! The king! Go on!'

'Then the feast began, and the pipers started to play, and such food they brought in! Oh, Gwennol, it was all decked out like a May-Day procession with flowers and frills. You'd think it couldn't be real food. But every plate of it was for eating. Then the king signed and the pipers stopped and the chief bard began to sing a love-lay. Oh, it was so sweet! And King Uther Pendragon stood up, with everyone watching him.'

Her cheeks were flushed like roses now, and I began to think I'd been wrong about it being Margawse, and I was all of a flutter. Even Margawse couldn't stop her telling her story now.

'He took his own knife, with the gold handle, from his belt and he kissed the blade. They'd set a swan before him, that seemed to be swimming in a lake of violets. He cut the first slice from the breast. And he laid that portion of honour on a golden platter and whispered to his steward. And everyone watched to see where the plate would be taken. It went past all the under-kings and queens on the high table. Past the benches just below them, with the fine dukes and duchesses, down our side of the hall.'

'And all the heads were turning, and only the king still smiling after the plate had passed people by. You never saw such long faces!'

'But I never thought. I swear I never thought it was coming to us.'

'Oh, Elaine. You ninny! The king's portion? You must have wanted it to be for you!'

'I didn't think of that, I was so busy watching. It came to our table and the steward stopped. It was like a dream. I was so silly. I thought he was going to give it to Father, to make up for not inviting him to sit on the high table.'

'Oh, *Elaine!*'

'And then . . . Gwennol! He put it down in front of . . . Mother!'

I was as stunned as she had been. They were both looking at me, those girls, laughing and frightened at the same time. But I couldn't take it in. I mean, I knew she was still a beautiful woman. But the High King himself!

'The noise, Gwennol! The stamping and the shouting.'

'The men were laughing, and the women were angry. It was wonderful.'

'And Mother went white, and then red, and white

79

again. And then I looked at Father, and I was frightened. He was furious.'

My eyes went to Ygerne then. She was staring across the room as if she was in a trance. There was just this little smile on her lips. When I saw that I could have slapped her face.

'Three times Uther sent her gifts. We'd never guessed. He must have fallen in love with her. The king, Gwennol!'

'The second time he gave her a golden goblet of wine, with a jewel in it. A little dragon brooch of red enamel and silver.'

'He smiled and lifted his drinking horn to her.'

'Then he sent sweetmeats in a casket of silver wire, all decked with lilies.'

'If I had been Father I would have killed him, then and there.'

A small, thin voice like the mew of a cat that's tasted blood. We'd all forgotten Morgan. She was crouched at the foot of the bed, her little white face peering up at us over the furs.

Her voice seemed to wake my lady out of a dream. All this time she'd sat there and never uttered a word. You'd have thought the Sisters had put a spell on her tongue. But when she spoke it hardly made sense.

'I thought it was all a dream. Lost with the Legions. But I have heard the tramp of the emperor's army on the streets. And the lays of the emperor's battles at the feast. And the hymns of the emperor's priest in the church.'

I don't know why, but that put me in a terrible temper. I was shaking with anger.

'And what's wrong with the British tongue, my girl? And the old straight track on the backs of the hills?

80

And a sky-roofed temple to worship our own gods as we've always done?'

But she didn't hear me. And I began to fear she'd tried to spell-speak Uther Pendragon and it had turned back on her. She wouldn't be the first that had happened to. Her eyes were miles away. And was it the past she was looking into or the future?

'I never knew that Britain was so wide or so fair. Day after day we rode. Past forests that seemed to have no beginning or end. Lakes like silver cobwebs in the morning sun. Corn springing green. And still when we lay down at night we were among our own. But the white dragon is cruel. They murdered Aurelius in his bed. And Uther has no wife to bear him sons. If he should fall . . .'

And then that little sharp voice, like claws scratching.

'What did Father do to Uther Pendragon?'

Chapter Eleven

Elaine seemed to be staring into the dark beyond the windows.

'Father sprang to his feet at the third gift, and his hand went towards his knife. Though he couldn't have struck the king in his own hall, could he?'

'I would have done,' cries Morgan.

'And then . . .'

'What? What did he do?'

'Nothing.'

'Tell her about the other man! The man in the archway.'

But Elaine wouldn't say a word more. I looked from one to the other of them. There was a queer look in Elaine's eyes. I've seen it in others. The look of those who can see more than they want to.

It was Margawse who rushed on. There was no stopping her now.

'There was a tall, thin man in one of the archways, on our side of the hall. No one seemed to have noticed him but Father, and then us, when we followed his eyes. He was about the same age as Uther Pendragon. Not too old. Not exactly handsome, because he had a crooked sort of face, but laughing. He was different from every nobleman in the hall. You could see it first in the way he was dressed. A plain white gown. But with a deerskin thrown over it, and the head left on and hanging down over his shoulder. But he wouldn't have been ordinary, even if he'd been wearing a toga or tunic and breeches like everyone else. He even made the king look a bit like a shadow, he was so . . . alive. He was the one who was holding Father from moving or shouting, I'm sure of it. And all he was doing was just crooking his hand a little and pointing a finger at him. And smiling that lop-sided smile. It looked as if Father was in a fit or a trance. I was sure he was going to fall down stiff on the floor at any moment. All we could see doing it was that one finger and his smile. But you felt as if there was a spider's thread between them, and Father was a struggling fly caught fast in it. Then I looked round at King Uther. And he was smiling back at the man. They had the same smile. As if they were brothers.'

'Who . . . was he?' I asked, and my tongue felt dry in my throat.

It was my Lady Ygerne who answered.

'Merlyn! Who else could it be? You guessed that, didn't you, Gwennol? Who here should recognise the Old Ones better than you and I?'

I'm not sure but that didn't give me the biggest shock of the evening, her coming out with it like that, in front of everybody. And I'm not just thinking of Margawse and Morgan, who were too young yet to be hearing about such things. I had the name through Cornwall of a powerful wise woman, and that suited me. And everyone knew I'd shown my lady some little skills of healing. But I'd taken good care they said no more than that about us. There are some names we have that are better not spoken. It's true there were not so many women in that room, but some of them were none of our side, and never would be. And she had spoken out loud a thing which we'd always kept secret, and which should have stayed so.

Emrys Merlyn. I'd known it must have been him, of course. And she'd seen I knew. I was just an old nurse on the cliffs of Cornwall and Merlyn was the king's soul-friend that was known for a great enchanter at the court. And what the two of us might have in common it wasn't for others to know. My mind was in a turmoil now. If I was right, and she had tried a charm to catch the king, she'd have met her match a thousand times over in Merlyn. Even the mighty Pendragons would dance to his tune. And where that dance might lead us now, if Merlyn was pointing his finger at us, I shuddered to think.

All the same . . . Not so old. Not exactly handsome. But laughing. It was not King Uther I hankered to see when they told me all the marvels of his court. I wasn't so old but I wouldn't dearly have loved to come face to face with Emrys Merlyn, just once in my life, though I doubted I'd have the courage to lift my eyes to his, and let him see there what I knew well he would. Well, the world's a stranger place than we have any notion of, and sometimes Fairyland may be closer than we think.

But I was still cross with my lady. If I'd have had my way I'd have sent the others all packing out of the room, and asked her straight out what she meant by it. She's not so old nor so grand that she can't remember me smacking her. But in that dun she was the Lady Ygerne and I was her children's nurse, and what could I say to her with all her waiting-ladies and serving-maids fussing round her?

So I said a bit shortly. 'Well, then. If the king's taken such a fancy to you, what are you doing galloping back here in such a lather before the feast of Easter's over, and acting as though the giants of St Michael's

Mount are on your heels with their cudgels?'

The two girls looked at each other then, as if neither of them dared to tell me what came next. So I
looked at Ygerne, and her face was red as a horse-
shoe from a smith's furnace. But she wouldn't bare
her shame to me.

'Is the thing so evil, then, that none of you are going
to tell me?'

I might have known it would be Margawse that
couldn't keep silent. It was the sort of folly that would
put a sparkle in her eyes. What was modesty to her?

'The next day the king did Mother even more
honour. We all went to church. And then ... Oh,
Gwennol, he was forever praising her beauty and
calling for his bard to make lays for her. He made her
walk beside him in the garden and cast petals on the
paths in front of her. And when the evening came, he
led her with him to the high table, while Father was
left with us, halfway down the hall. Afterwards, when
there was dancing and singing, we heard ... Elaine
and I heard . . . they were saying on our table . . .'

She broke off into giggles. Shameless, she was. As if
I hadn't lived long enough in a man's world to guess
what was coming next.

'They said ... everyone was whispering it ... the
king was having a bower prepared, next to his own
bed-chamber. And he'd had it filled with flowers, and
silks, and perfumes, and silver mirrors. And guess
who it was for? Mother!'

Poor silly woman. Couldn't she have seen the way
the wind was blowing, long before it got to that? She'd
lived long here in Bossiney, with only a handful of
Cornish lords and a white-robed priest for company.
But she'd feasted in kings' courts too. She wasn't as
green as all that.

I looked her straight in the eye.

'And what did you do?' I asked. 'When you found that out?'

'What any loyal wife would do. I told my lord,' she said, with her eyes cast down. Very demure, she looked. 'He was in a terrible rage. He called our people together. He had to keep his voice low, but he was so angry it was as if he was yelling to heaven. He ordered the men to saddle our horses in the dark and bring out our chariot. Of course, Uther's grooms went rushing to tell the king we were going, so Gorlois had them killed, every one, and the guards at the gate too. Even the yard-hounds he killed. So we rode out into the night, like thieves. But Gorlois went back towards the palace with his sword drawn, and Jordan and Britael with him. When we looked round there was a bright light in one of the doorways. Merlyn was standing there. He didn't say anything, Gwennol. He didn't do anything. He just stood and smiled. He has a terrible smile. And Gorlois turned like a man sleepwalking, and came back to us and mounted his horse. When morning broke, we were galloping as hard as we could for the west and Cornwall. And who knows if Uther Pendragon is coming after us now, with half the troops of Britain at his back?' There was a catch in her voice somewhere between sobbing and laughing, so that I couldn't be sure if she was sorry about it.

'Let him cross the Tamar if he dare. He won't rouse Cornishmen to do you wrong. They'll fight for my lord, never you fear,' I told her stoutly.

'Ah, you say that now, Gwennol. But you don't know Uther Pendragon. And he has Merlyn behind him. Uther's not like other men. There is something about him that makes even kings follow him. And love him too. I've seen it in their eyes at court. You don't understand, Gwennol. Even a Cornishman would find it hard to say no to him.'

And a Cornish woman too, I thought to myself. So that's how the land lies. And little you care that good men will have to die for this. And so I told her.

'Lucky for me,' I said, 'that my man is dead, and never gave me sons. There'll be many a woman weeping before this is over.'

But I judged her too hardly. She was right. I hadn't set eyes on Uther Pendragon – or on his soul-friend, either. It would have taken a stronger woman than her to have refused the glamour of that pair. But for all that, I'll swear she was never unwilling. And what I'll never know is who began that magic. Was it just the little spell she made that called him all the way to Cornwall? Or were there bigger powers than that at work already, to get her to make that boy the bards sing of? Either way, I should have known better than to meddle with them.

That little voice came again.

'Is Merlyn our enemy then?'

I didn't care to answer that. I left the child sitting on the floor, watching us.

We got Ygerne to bed, and her waiting-woman, Ruan, made ready to sleep with her, and by the time I looked round, Margawse had gone. The times I've wished my Lady Ygerne had given me a brood of boys to nurse! I should have been shot of them to their foster-fathers long before this. I went puffing out into the dark to look for her. And sure enough, there she was with some of my lord's young warriors, in the torchlight by the stables, laughing and as excited as her mother. And I don't doubt she was giving them a version of the story a sight more colourful than the one she had told me. I scolded her to bed and left her frightening Elaine with talk of battles coming.

And then there was Morgan to look for. She wasn't in her mother's chamber. I didn't need to go far. I knew I should find her with her father. He, poor man, had drunk himself stupid over the great table in the hall, with the pick of his warriors and house-servants watching by him. And there was Morgan, under the table, curled up asleep beside his feet like a puppy. I got old Sulian, that had seen more battles than any of them, to help me lift her, and she stirred in her sleep and cried out. She seemed heavy for such a skinny little thing, 'til we swung her clear of the table and a great sword fell out of her hand. It was no magic present from the king's palace. Only Gorlois's own sword that she had been clutching while she slept.

'No, no,' I scolded her gently. 'It will take more than you to save his life now.'

Chapter Twelve

I don't think any of us got much sleep that night, except my lord, though he never went to bed at all. It was a grey, misty sort of dawn, and chilly, too, for the year was still early. And so quiet. Even the birds seemed as if they were listening. There wasn't a sound from outside, and nobody dared to unbar the gate until my lord gave the order. He slept on, with his head on the table and his beard all wet in the spilled wine.

I huddled close in my shawl as I went to get water for my girls to wash. At least they would die proud and clean. Elaine was shivering and complaining, but then she always did. She wrapped herself in her fur robe and ran away to her mother to find some comfort. I had a fight with Margawse to strip her of her shift.

'Come on, my lass. You'll never make a fine queen with a dirty neck.'

By the time I had towelled her dry, her eyes were sparkling.

'Will there really be a war between the king and Father? Will Uther bring his whole army here to fight us? And all because of Mother?'

'You can wipe that smile off your face. Fighting means dying. And how do you expect your father to stand against King Uther Pendragon and all his fine warriors? If it ends the way I think it will, you'll be laughing on the other side of your face.'

Morgan stripped down to her skinny white body without needing to be told. She didn't smile, and she didn't shiver. You'd have thought the cold had no power over her if you hadn't seen the goose-pimples on her. She washed more carefully than usual, then dressed herself and fastened her girdle tightly. I looked down at her proudly. Even then, she was more of a queen than Margawse. I wondered what would become of her if her father died.

The night had cooled my lady down, and she was frightened now. There are few that can feel romantic in the cold grey of the morning. Now that she was more sensible, I felt kinder towards her. Poor lady, who had thought herself almost ready to be a grand-mother. And then to be courted by a king as though she was a handsome young princess. It was enough to turn any woman's head.

And so we all waited for my lord to wake up. Young Keby came by and saw me standing in the door of my lady's bower.

'What did I tell you?' he grinned. 'I said there'd be trouble if he took Lady Ygerne with him to court. I wouldn't mind having it off that one myself, even if she is old enough to be my mother. You can see she knows a trick or two. And Uther Pendragon can spot a good lay when he sees it, by all accounts. I reckon the king'll be standing in that doorway where you are before the week's out, or he's not the man they say he is. How's that for far-sight, Gwennol?'

'You cheeky devil,' I said. 'You want to watch that tongue of yours, or you won't have one much longer. My lady will hear you.'

But it was not her I was worrying about. All the

time I was casting my eyes about to see where
Morgan might be hiding herself.

'She'll be all right. It isn't her throat he'll be cutting,
is it? It's the likes of you and me that will catch it in
the neck if we stand in his way.'

But he was always a brave lad, Keby, for all he was
cheeky. And he was true to his lord and lady to the
end.

It was mid-morning when Gorlois walked out of the
hall. The men stopped whatever they were doing and
looked at each other, wondering who dared speak to
him first. But they hadn't made my lord Duke of their
war-hosts for nothing, and the morning had made a
man of him again. He sent riders to the east to find if
there was any news of King Uther coming. And others
he sent south and west, to his kinsfolk and his friends,
to call them to fight with him for his wife's honour
against the king, if need be. And when the messengers
had ridden away, the gate was barred again, though
it was broad daylight. We couldn't see out unless we
climbed on the ramparts, and all we could hear was
the honing of swords and the clang of hammer on iron
from the smithy-end.

My lady talked a long time to Lord Gorlois. She was
no fool, once she'd gathered her wits about her again,
now she was away from the glamour of the king's
palace. It made me feel better, for it should have
taken more than vanity to turn the head of a wise
woman, though she was of the lesser sort. But whatever she'd done, she'd have met more than her match
in magic there, as my lord was likely to meet his
match if it came to a battle.

By and by the sun came out, and we all began to feel
a bit safer, with so many men busying themselves for
war around us. It was foolish, really. What could they

do? But I've seen a sick child stop crying just to hear its mother sing a lullaby, though she can't save its life.

Morgan followed at her father's heels. She was quieter than usual, seemingly listening and thinking. Once she came running back to me, full of questions.

'Is this all because of Mother? Is she as beautiful as that? More beautiful than any woman in Britain? I never wanted to look like her.'

Which was just as well, seeing her hair was as black as a luck-cat's.

'She's beautiful, yes. And I don't mean just what you're supposed to say about any noble's wife. She scarcely looks older than the day she married your father. They say she's the handsomest woman in all Dumnonia, that I do know. Though I dare say they're only counting the gentry.'

'And is it so very important to be beautiful? Kings would really go to war because of it? Against their own friends? Father was Uther's friend, wasn't he, last year?'

'King Uther Pendragon would, by all accounts. And he's the only High King we have between us and the Saxons.'

'I used to want to be a king,' she said thoughtfully. 'But perhaps it's more powerful to be a beautiful woman. What do you think, Gwennol? If I was beautiful, would kings go to war because of me?'

I couldn't help laughing, for, much as I loved her, she was a sharp-faced, ugly child. If she had power, it would come from somewhere else.

'Handsome is as handsome does, my fine young lady. And if you want to grow up beautiful, like your sister Elaine, you'd better start drinking up your milk and put some flesh on those sparrow-bones of yours.'

She didn't heed me.

'So my father has the most beautiful woman in all Britain for his wife. Even King Uther Pendragon envies him. You can buy horses and jewels, but you can't buy somebody else's wife. You can only steal her. So Father must fight to guard her. She belongs to us. We won't let the Pendragon take her away from Cornwall.'

That surprised me. It had never struck me that she cared much about her mother 'til then. All the shine in her eyes was for her father. But she was proud like him. And when she saw her mother was a lady that a king might covet, she began to look at her in a new light.

Ygerne was with my lord, walking the ramparts and arguing about what they should do if the king sent for her. Morgan went back to them. And she stood looking at her mother as though she had never seen her properly before. As a man may look at a mare that he's thinking of buying. And presently I saw her walking behind them. She wasn't dancing about, but copying my lady's steps. And she was twisting her hair in her fingers as though she was thinking of braiding it with pearls as my lady did. Her father looked round then and saw her. He thought she was playing. He grinned through his beard and tossed her up in the air. But Morgan didn't shriek with laughter at him as she used to. She let him put her down. Then she smiled at him like a grown woman, and studied her mother closer than ever.

We hadn't long to wait.

95

Chapter Thirteen

I don't know what I expected. The fairy troops of
Gwyn, with their silver helmets, galloping out of the
mists to snatch us all away. Or the Black Hunt
screaming down on us in the darkness on their night-
hags, while we lay shivering with our faces turned to
the walls. Or those old Romans my granny used to tell
of, that stood in squares like human walls, fighting
and falling without ever moving a foot.

Not normal human beings anyway. Not like our
fighting Cornishmen, grinning through their beards
and brandishing their long swords, bragging and
showing off like men anywhere. I couldn't square that
with what I'd heard of Merlyn.

Well, I did what I could while we waited. Gorlois
wouldn't let me leave the dun, and that angered me. I
could have helped him more than most, and the gods
knew he needed it. It would take more than a strong
sword-arm and high courage to save him from this.
With Merlyn against us it needed nine times even my
strength to build the sort of rampart that had any
hope of keeping us safe. And even then I wouldn't
have trusted it to hold for long. But he wouldn't
budge, and I daren't tell him all I'd planned. I did go so
far as to threaten him, but he hardly seemed to notice
what I said. I wondered then if it was the beginning of
what I'd always feared. That one day he'd slip the

bonds I put on him before he married Ygerne. He'd
stop believing I had power. I could have shown him
then, before it was too late. I could have struck him
down. But I held my hand. He had troubles enough
coming to him as it was.

So I grumbled away and summoned Ygerne and
Elaine and two others that were wise among her
women. And do you know, my lady put her fine nose
in the air and told me she had more important things
to see to. Well, I'd spared Gorlois, but I was
sorely tempted to call a curse down on her, there and
then.

That left the four of us, and Elaine had been spoken
less than a year, though she was a sensible maid and
quick to learn. And nowhere for us to go but a grubby
lane behind the kitchen, where anyone might chance
upon us. The Mothers forgive me, I set Morgan on the
corner to give us warning. I built a fire, and we did
what we could. A little patterning. A handful of herbs
on the flames. A cock killed. But it was poor, thin
stuff, and we knew it. All the time I had this sick
feeling in my stomach that if this was all the strength
we could manage, it might do us more harm than
good. But I was like Gorlois. I had to try.

After that, there was nothing but waiting. I don't
mind admitting I was almost glad Gorlois hadn't let
me go where I meant. It's not much of a wall around
Bossiney. It wasn't built for war. But it felt a good
deal safer than walking out there on the cliff, with the
gulls slipping on the wind over the rocks and nothing
but thin air between you and the sea. A cold, lonely
place to be caught by what I feared was coming.

And yet. It's a funny thing, but I found my blood was
beating faster, like all the rest. And I can't swear it
was an unpleasant feeling entirely. I'd lived too much

in the old songs and stories. When the world was all
battles and magic and high deeds, and things turned
upside down for pride or love, and kingdoms lost and
won. All of a sudden we found we were living in such
a story, and I don't think there was one of us that was
wholly sorry, for all the evil that we guessed would
come of it. We'd all rather that something happened
to us than nothing. So we watched the skyline with
our hearts in our mouths. And whether we hoped or
dreaded what we might see, it's not for me to say.

But it wasn't much when it came. Three riders, or
so it looked. A little after noon next day. They rode
lighter than my lord and lady, without chariots. It's a
wonder they hadn't overtaken our people on the road.
But then, they didn't know the ways into Cornwall.
They weren't winging straight homeward, like swans
at evening. Or maybe they had reasons for not hurrying. Maybe it suited them to let the birds flock back
to Bossiney. It gave them a chance to ride right up to
our walls, and look around, see how the land lay and
where a strong king's army might do most damage if
my lord proved stubborn. Was it the vixen they
wanted, or her earth as well? There was one at least
that looked long and shrewdly round him before he
left us.

They'd ridden hard, but not so fast the horses had
foundered. They stood for a while where we had all
been looking for them. That little nick where the road
comes over the hill from the north-east. We never
doubted who they were or why they had come.

They stood so still those first few moments, you
might have thought three new pines had sprouted
over there on the ridge. They looked hardly human.
With the bright air behind them it seemed almost as if
you could see through them. Then they moved, and we

99

saw the glint of their armour, and knew then what we had to deal with.

Morgan caught her father's hand.

'Fight them, Father! We will never give in to them as long as we live.'

He just gripped her fingers. I heard her gasp. I don't think he even knew he'd done it.

They started to trot down the hill, and it was so still I could almost swear I heard their harness chiming like bells, though I couldn't have done. You'd think we'd never seen horsemen before. We were all of us on the walls and staring at them as if we couldn't move. Every soul in the dun was there – my lord and his wife and daughters, right down to the smallest slave baby in its mother's arms. Yet there wasn't one voice raised, not even Gorlois's. Just a sort of low murmur, like the sea on shingle under a fog. We were all holding our breath, to see if Uther and all his army were coming over the skyline behind them.

Looking back on it, I don't know why we didn't let her go there and then. We were beaten before we started. But they were high-blooded folk, and I suppose it had to be done the way it was.

We watched them come, and there was just enough dust on the road to hide the horses' legs so that they seemed to be swimming towards us on a brown tide. All this time the cows in the meadow outside the walls went on tearing at the sweet grass. They weren't thinking what might redden it before long. Though our own horses, that we'd picketed inside the dun, began to lift their heads and prick their ears.

Then I gave a great start. There was another rider had come over the hill. It wasn't the whole host of Uther Pendragon, but I don't think it could have shaken me more if it had been. Just one man. There

wasn't even a flash of armour on him. As soon as I
realised that I knew who it must be. And I couldn't
take my eyes off him. He rode alone and slowly on a
white horse. And as he drew near, I saw that he was
dressed fantastically. A great cloak that seemed to be
made of rags, every colour of the rainbow. And his
hair white with lime. That made me shiver. I'm not
lying when I tell you this: I felt his power, even from
where I stood. And something worse than that. I felt
sure that power had picked me out, even where I
stood packed in amongst all the others. Old Gwennol,
the children's nurse. And yet I swear he knew me. My
knees were trembling like weak brawn, but I was as
drawn to him as a magpie to a silver knife.

I had good reason to fear him, and he let me know it.
Halfway to the dun he stopped his horse, at the far
edge of our pasture, where the Great Oak grows. He
got down and he was a younger man than I'd
expected, even after Margawse had told me. He
strolled under those huge branches, and he laid his
hand on the bark of the trunk as familiarly as you
please and tilted his head back to look up at the
crown. He lifted his hand in a sort of salute. Even
from here I could swear his crooked face was smiling.
Well, I'd never in my life dared touch any oak-tree
like that, as if we were friends. Never mind that
one.

Suddenly I heard noise all around me. I'd only had
eyes for one man, but the rest of them had been
watching those three in front. Poor, silly fools, as if
the danger that threatened us was steel and iron.
Men can't see further than a sword and a shield, and
most women aren't much better. And all at once the
newcomers weren't ghosts or noontime shadows.
They were flesh and blood, with men's faces we could

see clearly and sweating horses under them. One of them carried a herald's staff.

They were still a good bowshot from the gate when Gorlois leaped down off the wall into the yard, with everybody tumbling down after him. I must have been the last, except for the sentries and a few boys that couldn't take their eyes off a coat of mail. I was always slow. But I was slower that day than I need have been. To tell you the truth, I didn't want to turn away. And it wasn't soldiers I was watching. I'm past bothering with them. Dangerous he may have been, but turning away from him was like being dragged out of a dream into a rough, cold world. And at the same time I was mortally afraid that the gate would open and he'd ride in, and I should have to meet him, eye to eye.

Well, such a to-do there was everywhere, I almost laughed at them when I saw it. Gorlois packed Ygerne and the three girls off into the bower out of sight, and barred the door after them, as if they were mares on heat, which in a way they were. Well, three of them, anyway. Morgan made a fuss, but he wouldn't listen to her. He set warriors with spears everywhere, lined up by the gates and all the way to the hall, and he was shouting for his best mantle and the clasps of silver and garnets, and polishing up his scabbard on the skirt of his own tunic. Pride. The sheer foolish pride of the man, flaunting his jewels and weapons at them, as he'd flaunted his wife at Uther Pendragon. I must have stood gaping like a fool. Next thing I knew I was bundled into the sleeping-hut. They almost threw me on the floor and the door slammed shut behind me. This was to be men's work, seemingly. There wasn't a woman left in sight.

I got to my feet as quick as I could and hobbled back

to the window. I couldn't see them open the gates, but they seemed to swing back as if a giant's hand had pushed them. It was so bright over the sea it made me blink my eyes. All the same, even while my sight was dazzled I knew Merlyn hadn't come. I should have felt it in my blood.

Uther's three messengers dropped from their horses. Their legs had that wearisome roll of men who have ridden hard and long. But they were proud and haughty under their dirt, even so. Their leader was a proper lord this time. They told me afterwards his name was Ulfin, he that stood as close friend to Uther as Jordan was to Gorlois. I should have studied that face while I had the chance. I'd be seeing it closer than I wanted to . . . if you could call it seeing. But then, I just watched the fine flash of their cloaks go by me as they walked through our spear-guard into the hall. Then we all had to wait.

After a while I couldn't help myself. I found a stool and clambered up higher on it. I couldn't see much over the stockade even then. But there was a place where the headland reared up above the rest of the cliff. A green mound, caught between the top of the wall and the sky, that I knew was sweet with wild flowers if you could see it closer.

He was there, with a deep blue sky behind him, and the sunlight glistening on his white hair and his coloured ribbons. Sitting on a white horse among the walls of the old people you can still see in the grass. He could have come straight out of Fairyland. But I didn't doubt for one moment he was real, and here in Bossiney now. I think it was the rest of the world I'd have doubted first.

They were carrying wine into the hall now. The best jars too, that they said had come all the way from

103

Palestine. Gorlois would make a fine show of polite-
ness, though there was a dusty answer at the bottom
of the cup. We knew what Uther's men had come for,
of course. Our Gorlois had insulted him, good and
proper, leaving his court without permission and killing his people. He'd ordered him back to London with
his lady, on pain of death. We knew what message
they'd take back with them, too. Still, a guest's a
guest. Gorlois wouldn't have the king say that he
hadn't shown them hospitality first.

Our men on guard shuffled their feet and growled
as they waited, but the birds in the trees were singing
away now as though they hadn't a care in the world.

The king's party came out at last, and walking
quicker than before. They looked angry, though I
can't think what they had expected. But perhaps it
was just a show they had to put on for honour's sake. I
often think that so much that happened that year was
play-acting. It's always like that with the nobility.
Common people like us say what we think, or show it
in our faces. Like children.

And that made me gasp all of a sudden and turn my
thoughts for the first time that day to Morgan. She
was still young enough to wear her heart naked in her
face. Even without being told I knew she'd be watching
from the window of her mother's bower. I wondered
what she'd seen. I scrambled back on my stool and let
Uther's warriors ride out with their backs to Bossiney
and our fate in Gorlois's answer. I hadn't time to look
after them. My eyes went straight to the downs.

There was no horseman any more up on that mound
of turf above the sea. The place looked as empty then
as ever I've seen it. Merlyn had gone.

And you young ones may laugh at this. You think the
blood runs cold when you're past fifty. But I tell you

this. I never felt such a loss when my own man was gone and I lay alone month after month. It was so bad that moment I had to pull up my skirts and thrust my own finger into my blood-hole to satisfy myself, and never mind who heard me crying. Afterwards, I was ashamed. It had been too small a thing for what I felt.

I couldn't tell you if Morgan saw him or not.

Chapter Fourteen

I don't know why she did it. It's a thing I can't forgive. She went to Nectan, and not to me. Ygerne, that I'd sung lullabies to in the old tongue before she could speak her mother's name. Ygerne, that I'd taken into the woods showing her leaves and roots even before she knew the power of them. Ygerne, that coaxed me to use a deep charm of mirrors and apples to bring young Gorlois to her door. Ygerne, that I'd whispered into the old way, having no little maid of my own. Did she think I'd failed her, bringing her nothing but daughters?

I chided her to help me build a wall. She just stared at me, with her blue eyes very round.

'They say his parents wore the Roman purple.'

'Rome's gone. Uther Pendragon's flesh and blood. He's king over us only as long as the Britons want him. He can be killed, whatever his father wore.'

'But it wasn't just his father, Gwennol. His *mother* wore purple too.'

And what did she mean by that? I should have seen the way her hopes were turning.

Well, as soon as the gate was opened again she was off. Just her and Ruan, in plain cloaks and hoods. Gorlois was in a fury when he found out. It would be days yet before Uther got his message, like a slap in the face. But he wasn't going to have his prize running

107

loose over the countryside like any milkmaid. He sent Jordan and Britael galloping after her. But they were too late.

It wasn't far from us to the coombe where the saint lived. A sweet, rocky valley, it is, with the river rushing over the stones, cool and green, and the trees and ferns hanging over the water. And then you come on it suddenly. A great hole in the rock, as if a giant had punched his fist through it. And a white spout of water flinging itself down through it into a pool. They knew how to pick their spots, those Christians. He'd made his hut there, and grew his little garden of herbs and kept a few fowls. Just for the eggs. They say he wasn't man enough to kill one.

I'd been there once, when curiosity got the better of me. Just to see what we were up against. I didn't get close. I was still coming through the hazel trees when he heard me. He'd been sitting on a mossy stone out in the water with his long shanks dangling in the stream, and singing to himself or his god. But I hadn't set foot in his clearing before he'd whipped round and was on that bank and snatched up his staff where it was lying in the grass. I thought for a moment he was going to beat me with it. But he just held it at both ends, stretched out like a bar between us. His blue eyes burned and words came out of his mouth. Hard-edged, like steel. Latin, I suppose it was. I couldn't understand it. But I knew what he meant, all right. I don't think he cursed me. I didn't take any pain from it. But I couldn't stir one step forward from where I stood, do what I would. I never tried again.

But it wasn't his staff that stopped Jordan and Britael, so I've heard. It was the sight of my lady, standing among the primroses beside the water, with her hands lifted, praying. Think of that: the wise

108

Ygerne of Cornwall and a bloodless Christian hermit.
It made me spit like a cat. What was she, that he'd let
her into his holy ground when he'd barred me? I'll tell
you what she was. False. For all the power I'd given
her, she'd swing from one side to the other where she
thought it would do her most good. Though what help
she thought she'd get from a childless man like that is
more than I can say. And I dare say he thought she
was a lamb come back to the fold. She was a wise
woman, all right. There was none of us truly knew
what was in her mind.

When they'd done their prayers, he put his hands
on her head, and she crossed hers over her breast
and cast her eyes down very modestly, or so Ruan
said. Then she walked over to her husband's men,
very meekly. And Britael set her on his horse and led
her home. Gorlois raved at her, but she never
answered him. Just stood before him with her head
bowed down and a little smile on her lips. When he'd
blown himself out she said just one thing.

'I have prayed, my lord, for the safety of Britain.'

I could have wished I'd had Gorlois for a son,
instead of that one for a daughter.

But she was as false to Nectan as she was to me.
Elaine was missing a long time that night, and when
she came back she wouldn't meet my eye. It didn't
take me long to know what the two of them had been
up to behind my back.

I was sick of the lot of them. If they didn't want my
help they could seethe in their own cauldron. Why
should I burn my fingers plucking them out of the
stew? So I stayed where I was. I never called the wise
even then. I had messengers as swift as any of
Gorlois's. I could have summoned a host that was
stronger than his. Our weapons are different but they

109

can shield and kill as surely as metal and wood. I let them lie. Many a time I've grieved over that. I was so angry with Gorlois and Ygerne, I never thought what might happen to Morgan.

Before evening the first of Gorlois's messengers came galloping back, and the news was as cold as the sea-wind that was beginning to rattle the thatch. All next day it was the same tale. It seemed all the chieftains of Cornwall had gone off to that Easter crown-wearing and there was no one left who dared to raise a sword against the Pendragon.

'They'll come back to the west now the feast is done with. My kin will fight for my honour. Blood of my blood. Sword-brothers and father's friends.'

Oh, yes, I thought to myself. Who are you fooling? For which of our chieftains of Cornwall can't count more enemies than friends? Fat cattle stolen. A daughter dishonoured. A son killed in his cups. The gentry know no other way of passing their time but fighting and boasting and raiding. Gorlois had as ready a sword as any of them. And they've long memories in these parts. Our duke couldn't rally heart and hand across the country now. They'd fight for him against the Saxons, but not against Uther. He hadn't Merlyn's glamour round him.

Yet I don't think it even occurred to him to let Ygerne go. Not though this Uther Pendragon claimed to be High King over us all to the Land's End, and Gorlois was only war-lord of Cornwall. I think he knew she fancied Uther. It was that that stuck in his pride. It made him angrier than I'd ever seen him before. He didn't shout and bluster. It was a deep, dark anger, that turned him in on himself. Oh, he'd had fights a-plenty. Cattle-raids, pirates, Saxon wars. But he was always laughing in his beard beforehand as if it were some great sport. And when enough blood was spilt and enough armour dented and enough booty snatched from whoever wasn't quick enough to hide it, both sides would break and ride away. And they'd fill their heads with ale and raise a lament over their dead and in the same breath be planning the next raid.

He wasn't laughing now. He'd fight this battle to the bitter end. He'd see every last one of us dead before he let her go.

But he still had one dagger up his sleeve.

There was a shout from the sentry at the gate, and we all jumped like hares. But Gorlois grinned.

'Let her in,' he cried, and strode across the yard with us crowding after him.

It was no horseman this time, sweating back through bogs and forests to bring us bad news. It was a woman we saw marching in through the gate. Well, three women, to tell the truth, for she'd brought two of her nuns with her. Bryvyth, who'd built her nunnery on Tintagel Head. She had a tall staff in her hand, curled at the top like a shepherd's crook, a white wool gown over a linen smock, and bare feet. She'd cut her hair, and you might think from all I've said that she was a slave. But you'd never have thought that if you'd seen her. Her way's not mine but I can tell those that have power from those that haven't, and she had it. She wouldn't look a man in the face if she could help it, and she kept her head covered for modesty. But she had a way of folding her arms that was as bold as if she'd looked him straight in the eye. She was a big woman, too.

'You sent for me. Is the business so urgent that your man must come yelling at my gate while we're singing in chapel?'

'I've reason enough to rouse the whole of Cornwall.'

'So I hear. And what has Gorlois's quarrel to do with the nuns of Tintagel?'

'It has everything. Uther wants my wife, and he shall not have her. When he hears my answer, there will be an army in Cornwall. I must have a fortress to fight from.'

'The Duke of Cornwall has many strongholds. Did you call me here to tell you which one to pick?'

He moved quickly then, and we thought he was going to strike her. But he caught his hand back.

'Bryvyth Crook-Staff, you may be a woman but you are a learned one, and no fool. There is one place, and one place only, that could hold out against such a war-host: Tintagel.'

We must have all drawn our breath sharply then, like a nest of adders. It was no more than everyone must have thought in their minds many a time. That rocky island, with the sea coming at it on all sides. And just one neck of rock, so high above the waves it made you dizzy, joining it to the land. What chieftain mustn't have envied it for a fortress, these hundreds of years? But if we thought it, it was never spoken. For everyone knew Tintagel was a woman's place. First ours, now theirs. It had a name: the strong place where the two waters meet. There were few standing there that understood the meaning of that, or guessed how it was used. But the men kept away. Why else had those nuns chosen to set their cross there?

'You are thinking that Uther Pendragon would respect sanctuary? A king that would violate a Christian wife?'

'I'm not asking you for sanctuary, woman. I want a fort! A hundred warriors. Three lines of ramparts.

Ten men alone might hold that bridge for me against half of Britain.'

She had a temper like his. She raised her staff to him then, like a bar across a door.

'On your knees, godless man! Shame, that you should even think of it. There's one way only Gorlois will come to Tintagel – when he brings his lady wife to me for sanctuary. No warrior passes our wall bearing weapons, nor ever shall. If Uther Pendragon comes, it will be Bryvyth Crook-Staff will meet him on the bridge. But Gorlois, war-lord of Cornwall, will have to fight his bloody battles somewhere else.'

She didn't wait for him to argue. She turned her back and strode out of the gate with her nuns after her. She never once looked back.

Gorlois had a face like thunder. We feared he'd send the guards and have her struck down before she'd reached the downs. But he let her go. There were only a dozen nuns on Tintagel, and a handful of schoolchildren. But whether it was her he was most afraid of, or the place, Gorlois never tried to take it from them by force.

Chapter Fifteen

Still we sweated. And I soon feared it wasn't only Ygerne that had been spell-struck, up there in London. Gorlois was like a fly trussed in a cobweb. He'd had this one idea, and Bryvyth had thwarted him. Now he didn't seem to know what to do.

That frightened me. It wasn't like him, that was always so quick to leap on his horse and draw a sword. Bossiney's no place for war, but Gorlois had forts enough on the hilltops, above the forests. Chilly, windswept old crags. They weren't the sort of places you'd want to live in, when you could have sweet grazing on the downs and good fishing in the sea. But that's where we should have fled by now. That's what they were built for, in the old times, when it was clan against clan and we hadn't a king over all Dumnonia or a Saxon army to turn our thoughts elsewhere. Gorlois was known for a canny war-lord, but there wasn't the youngest kitchen-maid couldn't see that we should be somewhere else but where we were. And my courage seemed to fall into my boots, for I guessed who'd done this to him, and there'd be worse to come.

His warriors didn't like it one bit either. They buzzed loud enough. I saw Jordan and Britael arguing with him, and old Sulian trying to steady the younger bloods.

'Why doesn't Uther come?' says Margawse. 'What is he doing?'

You'd think she wanted us murdered. She was always impatient, that one, whether it was good or ill coming.

'Let's hope he's changed his mind. Maybe he's put up a doe that will make sweeter hunting than your dear mother,' I told her.

I glanced round at Ygerne as I said it. She tossed a braid over her shoulder and looked away as though she hadn't heard me, so that I couldn't tell if she liked the thought or not.

'He could be in Cornwall by now,' said Tudy. 'Wouldn't he take the high road over the moors to make for the forts? The Pendragon's a man of war. He'd never think we'd be such fools as to stay in Bossiney, like cattle at Samain, waiting to be butchered.'

That struck home. There was a loud growl ran round from near a hundred men. Gorlois had been sitting hunched over the fire, staring into the flames. But when he heard that he straightened up and gazed at Tudy, round-eyed as an owl. But even then we never guessed what was in his mind.

'Maybe he's come to his senses and gone off to fight Picts or Saxons instead of good Cornishmen,' Keby said.

'It's a long march from London,' Sulian tried to warn us. He was the oldest warrior Gorlois had, and he'd fought in many a battle against the Saxons. 'And the Pendragon will have an army to muster if he wants to besiege us. Likely enough it will be Pentecost before he crosses the Tamar.'

'Not he,' said Jordan. 'There were warriors enough came with their lords to the feasting to make a fair old war-host. He hadn't got halls big enough to hold us all. There were camp-fires burning in every market-place and tumbledown temple the Romans had left. My lady may have turned his head but Uther's a soldier. He's not so mad with love he wouldn't have the sense to keep those spears about him 'til he got my lord's answer.'

We came to Sunday. And still we hadn't moved from that round in the meadows, where an army could march right up to our gate, and nothing to stop them. I'd tried what I could to rouse Gorlois with nails and thorns and more besides. But he'd gone beyond my reach by then.

It struck me folk were a sight keener to go to chapel that morning than ever they'd been before. There hadn't been such a crowd gathered round it since the day Nectan came striding up from the beach with his psalm-book on his back and his bell in his hand.

My lady was there inside, of course, fresh as a girl at her first communion. I'd love to know what was hatched between those two, and what they'd prayed for.

The nuns came trooping along from Tintagel Island too, singing as though their God was still in his heaven. They were the only ones that didn't look afraid. What had they to fear from Uther Pendragon? A religion for slaves, my mother used to call it. Nectan feeding us with bread, though he'd hardly a scrap of flesh on his own bones. Big Bryvyth in her housemaid's gown, serving us rich wine from a chalice set with jewels. But they'd caught more than slaves now. I glowered at them from where I stood. Morgan was standing beside me, singing away in her clear voice. I don't think she cared what the words meant, then. Her eyes were fixed on her father. He glared back at those two, and mostly at Bryvyth.

117

But it was Nectan he collared afterwards, speaking hoarse as though the words choked him.

'When Uther comes, I shall expect you to do your
duty as my priest. You cannot wield a sword, but you
can call down curses on our enemy.'

I've seen a bull's nostrils widen like Nectan's did
then. If I'd been Gorlois I'd have jumped well clear.

'Aye! The prayers of the Lord are more powerful
than pagan battle-axes. But do you think I would aim
them against a Christian prince?'

'Uther, Christian? A king that turns to a druid for
his soul-friend?'

'Emrys Merlyn is the son of a holy virgin. Who are
you to slander them both? You who keep a great witch
to teach your daughters!'

Gorlois swung round on me then and his eyes went
wide. I stood my ground and gave him back look for
look. Let him think what he would now. Then he gave
a great laugh.

'Old Gwennol! You'd compare her with Merlyn?
You haven't met him, man!'

But nothing he could do would shift the saint. There
wasn't one of them would give him what he wanted.
And when I turned round, there was Morgan, staring
at me like a little owl.

The time had seemed long, watching those empty
hills. Now, looking back on it, I could have wished it
had gone on for ever.

But Uther Pendragon was in more of a hurry than
we bargained for. And whether it was just my lady's
sweet face, or hot anger because Gorlois of Cornwall
had refused to hand over what he wanted, or whether
he'd noticed the first grey hairs frosting his beard,
it's not for me to say. He was a bold war-lord before,
and now he had Merlyn at his elbow. When his heralds

came back with Gorlois's dusty answer, I wouldn't
mind betting he had his saddlebags packed for war
already. Lord Gorlois was known to be a proud man
and Uther Pendragon was not a king to sit about waiting for an insult.

We watched Gorlois pace the ramparts, 'til the
stars started to prick through that April sky. He was a
dark man in daylight, and he looked darker then. I
should have been getting my girls to bed, but none of
us wanted to move. It was pretty near like waiting for
a sentence of death. I stood outside my lady's bower,
with my arms round Morgan. And she was stiller than
I was. Stiller than any child her age had a right to be.
Watching her father.

He turned his head suddenly and the watchman
gave a great cry, so we knew they were coming. Two
messengers came galloping in as hard as they could
ride. We didn't need to hear them shout.

'Uther has crossed the Exe. He'll be in Cornwall
tomorrow!'

That brought Gorlois back to life at last. He came
striding down the steps into the dun. The yard was
full of our shadows, crowding round him, like a town
of ghosts. We held our breath to hear what he would
do. We thought we knew the choice. To fight Uther
Pendragon and die, or give Ygerne over to him and be
shamed. We never guessed the madness that was
going through his brain.

He smiled at us, and played with his sword, so that
it clinked in his scabbard. It was the only sound in the
evening air, except for the sea far off that was like
our own breathing.

'I will not stay here!' he said harshly, like a man
condemned to die. 'I cannot fight him in the open
plain, and he knows it. Nor can I hold this house

against him. We shall march to Caer Dimiliock and make a stand there, 'til enough Cornishmen come to my aid to make a fair battle.'

And not before time, I thought, though it won't save you. Poor fool. Who but your own kin will fight for you now? There's a richer king than you coming, with glamour in his train and the promise of glory after for those who follow him against the Saxons. And what has Gorlois got to offer them now that he's out of favour?

Well, the men burst out cheering, of course. My lady was the only calm one among us. Win or lose, she didn't count on being harmed. She put her hand on his arm and smiled up at him.

'But Uther is on the road already. He may be close behind your scouts. What if he catches us before we reach Caer Dimiliock? Why can we not stay here and defend our own Bossiney?'

Oh yes. I could see the way her mind was shaping. Bossiney's a homely round. It's not one of your high rock forts that will stand months of siege. That wasn't what she wanted. A bitter, wasting war. Growing thin and scrawny like some hermit woman, to fall into Uther's hands when all her looks were gone. She wanted Gorlois to ride out to battle on our cattle pastures. She saw herself standing on the ramparts, watching two lords fight it out to the death over her, and she waiting to give herself to whichever of them won, like a prize at a fair. Ygerne the Beautiful. She'd been a virtuous wife, as I account it, but she was too much like Gorlois herself. She'd the same taste as he had for fame and fortune, but it took her a different way. So she turned white like the rest of us when she heard what he was planning.

'You will not ride the same road as me,' he said,

barking it out in the voice of a man who knows he is speaking folly but is not to be argued with. 'Dimiliock's strong. It can stand out for many weeks. Maybe Uther Pendragon will grow tired of dashing his head against Cornish granite for what he cannot have. But if I fall, he will find himself cheated of what he came to steal.'

Morgan caught her breath, sudden-like. There wasn't one of us understood him, even then. My lady said, in a strangled kind of voice, 'Then . . . where shall I be?'

We heard the waves far off beating at the foot of the cliffs and I think I was not the only one who saw the height of that drop in my mind and wondered how far Gorlois might go to cheat Uther Pendragon.

'Here!' he cried, and he laughed at last, like the old days, splitting his beard and grinning with his white teeth.

Morgan's was the only laugh that followed his, just as if this was some new game he'd thought of.

'Here? You'd leave me here for Uther Pendragon?'

'Three soldiers and a handful of servants. You won't need more. Tudy was right. Here's the one place he'll never dream of finding you. He'll think the place is deserted when he hears I've gone. He's High King of Britain. He'll go where there's a strong fort and a great war-host. You know that man's pride.'

She was terrified now.

'You're mad to leave us to his army!'

'No madder than he is, that thinks he can steal my wife.'

'But he ordered us back to the feast at London. You told him no. You defied him. His troops will burn every village, every dun, every farm, before they reach Caer Dimiliock. What if some of them come here without the king?'

121

Couldn't he see what she was trying to tell him? It wasn't falling into the Pendragon's hands that she was afraid of. There were those under him who wouldn't stop to ask her name.

He nodded to the warriors behind him. 'I'll leave you a faithful guard. Sulian, Tudy, Coan. They'll know what to do if you're found.'

If they hadn't been grey before those three would have changed colour then. Years now, they'd been too stiff in the elbow to ride to war with the rest. But there was only one stroke he wanted from them this time. I saw the men's hands drop away from their sword-hilts as if they'd been burned.

My lady gasped at that. She could see that he meant it. The words came rushing out of her.

'And what of your daughters? Would you have them killed too?'

That stopped him. I felt the muscles of Morgan's shoulders tighten under my fingers as we waited. Gorlois went white for a moment. He had no answer to that. He would have died himself and taken her with him if he had to, but not his daughters.

Ygerne seized her moment.

'At least send us somewhere safer than this,' she begged him. 'Let us go to the nuns on Tintagel Island as Bryvyth said. They'd give us sanctuary.'

That touched him on the raw. He swore at her then.

'There's only way I'll have you go to Tintagel now. If you hear Gorlois is dead, then shear your hair and take off your gown, and go to Tintagel with my daughters and take your vows as nuns.'

Well, we all looked at each other. We didn't know what to do. I stood clutching my little Morgan's body in front of me for dear life. I'll tell you, I was terrified. If I'd thought him spell-struck before, it was nothing to the madness that had bewitched him now.

But we were only women, and the men had been cooped up long enough. It was Jordan moved first. And then it was like a spark in the straw, and everyone shouting their heads off. It was coming on twilight, but in a moment the slaves were dashing about, emptying the storehouses, though dear knows we had little enough left that was fit to eat after that wet old winter. They were packing it all into panniers and carts. And the war-horses were whinnying as they threw the saddles on.

Ygerne just stood there dumbstruck, with Elaine and Margawse, and watched them bring two chariots out. Three of her women wrapped themselves in cloaks and climbed into them. And Britael lifted a little kitchen-maid into the second one, bundled up so she might have been Morgan.

All Gorlois's warriors mounted and lined up, before and behind, with a train of pack-horses loaded with all the gear they could carry.

I thought Gorlois was gone mad. But at the last he surprised me. He looked me straight in the eye and said, 'If they come near, Gwennol, try all you know. There's more things than morning mist that can deceive the eye, though I fear you've left it too late to gather your brood. Look after my daughters. Fight Merlyn any way you can.'

I hadn't heard his voice so gruff since his hound died. I just stood with my mouth hanging open like a fool. All those years, and maybe he'd guessed more than I thought. Morgan twisted her head back to smile at me, as though she'd always known.

I don't mind telling you, tears stood in my eyes. He was always a brave man. And it was all my doing. When he was just a young lord and whole of heart, I'd pared the apple that had brought him to Ygerne's gate. I put my hands on either side of his face and kissed his head. I felt my power going into his blood then. I couldn't save him. But he wouldn't go into the dark unblessed.

He hugged Morgan strongly to him.

'Be brave, little warrior. Look to the honour of my name.'

It was hard for him to say it. She answered him fiercely.

'Never you fear, Father. Whatever you hear shall make you proud of me.'

She buried her face against his breastplate, and I had to prise her off. But she didn't cry, though she must have known what that parting meant.

He kissed Margawse and Elaine, and whispered to them and fondled their hair. Even Margawse looked pale. And last of all he embraced Ygerne, long and hard. She didn't say a word.

Then he gave the order, and the column started to move. For a long while we heard the tramp of hooves and the creak of carts going past us. When the yard was quiet we scrambled up on the ramparts and watched them go, a host of shadows marching away in the twilight. But they scorned to hide themselves. As dusk turned into night we saw torches spring out and fire flashed red on their spears and armour. All up the hill there were rivers of lights moving. Gorlois's kin were hosting in the dark.

Then our men shut the gate, and we were left in an empty dun.

Chapter Sixteen

We didn't know if Uther would come on us in the dark,
as Gorlois had taught him that night at Mount Damen.
We were starting at every sound. There weren't
many of us, and we must have looked like a handful of
ghosts. My lady and her waiting-woman Ruan, the
three girls and myself, young Keby and a couple of
kitchen-women. And those grey old warriors, Sulian,
Coan and Tudy.

We daren't show a light. The dun was meant to look
hollow and deserted. If any nosy folk looked in next
morning, then we'd make ourselves out to be a parcel
of greybeards and slaves left behind to mind the
place, with all the glory and high blood gone somewhere else. But it was better no one saw us at all.

We moved into the great hall, where at least we
had straw and water and a little food left. I got the
slaves to fetch all the blankets they could find, and we
made ourselves ready for weeks of cold hiding. And
who could tell what would happen to us after that?

We couldn't use my lady's bower. That was supposed to be empty. But nothing that any of us could
say would persuade my lady to dress herself and
Gorlois's daughters like common peasant women,
still less shear themselves like slaves. She was a
brave woman, Ygerne, when all's said and done.
She'd meet her death if she had to, but it must be

125

nobly, like a duke's lady, not a kitchen-maid left behind. But I didn't think that dying was as much in her mind as it was in mine just then. And when you come to think of it, she had less need to fear death than the rest of us. There was just those three old men guarding her, and I could see that under their fine mail they were more nervous of what they'd been ordered to do than I was.

No. Ygerne would live, all right. She was what this whole game was about. She was a wise woman who would make shift for herself. When Uther Pendragon came, as come he must, Ygerne would be waiting for him, as beautiful as the day she walked into his feasting-hall and won his heart.

So she changed her dress as well as she could by starlight. She chose it even more carefully than she usually did. She had the decency not to put on her best feast-day robe. The dress she settled on was two years old, and faded with washing, but for all that it was a pretty thing and made her look not more than seventeen years old, and so Lord Gorlois had often told her. Sky-blue it was, by daylight, embroidered with roses and violets, and she tied a girdle of silver about her waist. She still had pearls in her hair. And she dressed her daughters finely too, though she had a tussle with Morgan. That one would rather have gone bare-legged in a coat of mail if anyone had let her. Over it all they put homespun cloaks of dun and russet, such as farmers' wives and daughters wear, with hoods for their jewelled hair. That was for outside only. It was no proper disguise. We all knew that in a twinkling of an eye they could throw them off and show themselves for what they were. Ygerne wouldn't pretend. And it was nothing but that black jealousy of Gorlois that stopped him seeing this was the only safe way.

126

Yes. There's the rub. Safe. That's the sort of word you and I would think of. I know it was mightily on my mind that long night. But it's not a word that men that are highborn have any use for. They live in some dream of pride and glory, so you'd think they had no fear of death like common folk. And they'd take wives and daughters with them to the grave, like slaughtered hounds, if they had to. A Christian, he called himself, and went to Nectan's chapel, but I hadn't noticed my lord was so very different from the old chiefs that the bards still sing of. I don't think he wished to be. And my lady had always kept one foot, and more, on the old road.

The moon rose late that night. And when it came I minded my lord's last pleading as well as I might. I knew I couldn't keep Uther Pendragon away from us, with Merlyn beside him, but I might yet be able to wrap us round in a Cornish mist so that some things might stay unseen a little while longer. This time I ordered Ygerne to help me and she didn't dare refuse now.

That was the night we whispered Margawse. We needed all the help we could get. But when she was joined to us, it couldn't be done proper. I often wonder if the Mothers were angry with us over that.

But Morgan we never spoke, either of us. Not even then.

I was for lighting a fire under the stars, the way it should have been done. Who would be awake to see us now? But Sulian wouldn't let me. He was a plain-thinking soldier that was more afraid of Uther than of me. So I paid that price for a promise that the men would keep their eyes shut and their backs turned. We sat cross-legged in the yard, under the half moon. I'd put Morgan to bed long ago. But I knew she hadn't

127

stayed there. I could feel her watching us through the dark doorway, like a cat at a mousehole.

I battled against Merlyn that night, as I hadn't dared do before. I should have saved my strength. I had left it too late.

Ygerne's heart wasn't in it. All the time I could see her eyes going over her shoulder, though you couldn't see anything above the ramparts but treetops and stars. She let her cloak fall open, showing her pretty dress, and she put up her hand in the moonlight to touch her hair and her white throat. Even as she chanted the words with me her look was far away. She never wanted to be invisible. It was a poor, weak circle we made, like trying to bind a giant with a daisy-chain.

But then, perhaps she was more sensible than us. How could those four ever hope to hide what they were from the king, with their high bearing and their soft white hands?

When it was done, it was almost daybreak. I stomped up to the ramparts in no good temper. For I knew already it had all been wasted effort, and it had left me tired. I let the sea-breeze blow on my face and I wished I was back in my childhood home in Polzeath and rid of the lot of them.

Then I felt a small, cold hand slipped into mine. Morgan was smiling up at me, as if she was trying to coax me into something.

It made my heart turn over, not for the first time by a long way. For she had a way of smiling, as though you were the only person that mattered in the whole world. And sorry I was for what I had been wishing to her and hers just then.

She squeezed my hand.

'That's not how it should be done, is it, Gwennol? Not like that. Not here.'

128

And her little lips were still smiling, but her eyes had gone very dark and bright, staring deep into mine.

'Where, Gwennol? Where is the power, really?'

My own eyes went sideways then, though I tried to pull them back. She followed where I looked. And I was pleased to hear her gasp. It wasn't everything she knew, at eight years old. And even then I didn't tell her all of it.

Tintagel Head. That proud stack of rock that was almost an island. Just that one narrow ridge from cliff to cliff that was more dreadful than any drawbridge. The nuns had got it now. It even looked a bit like a fort. There was a ditch and a bank dug in front of the bridge, and they'd put old Padern there in the porter's lodge. He lived alone, and he was the only man they'd let near them, and then only when there was heavy work to be done. But beyond the causeway it was as peaceful a scene as you could wish to see in an April dawn. The white walls of their little huts scattered about the grass like so many daisies, tucked into the ledges with their backs to the winter storms. The sheep grazing on the hilltop. And the stone cross above it all.

Well, they say they'd carved a cross on it. You couldn't see that from here. Just a shaft of stone pointing at the sky. I needn't tell you what it looked like to me.

So she didn't see my eye go downward. She was gazing like a child spellbound at what she thought I'd shown her. For I didn't give that nunnery more than a glance. My mind was seeing deeper than that. You'll know where I mean. On the beach below those cliffs there's a deep cleft, where a hand has reached inside the bowels of the land and plucked out a hollow way

129

right through the rock. Like a hole between two legs.
The sea comes washing in from either side. Even then
I thought I could hear the stallions of Manawydan
neighing.

I'd left Morgan still staring at the cross of the
nunnery with her eyes wide and startled. Well, she
wasn't wholly wrong, was she? Those white nuns
couldn't have lived where they did, and heard the
waves around them, lain in the night alone and still,
and not felt something of what went on beneath them.
And there were some who did more than that. Though
there was the devil to pay later when Bryvyth found
out.

So I let Morgan believe what she would that morning. In the end she knew the whole of it, better than
anyone.

'Couldn't we go there?' she said, very fierce. 'Can't
we go to Tintagel and make magic with them there?
Real, powerful magic.'

I shook my head.

'It's too late, my lover. I'm not stirring one foot outside these walls until this is past, and nor will you. We
must bide where we are, and use what strength we've
got, though it's little enough for what's coming
against us.'

'And Father?' she asked. She had a way of piercing
straight to the heart of things. 'Does he have those
with him who can make magic to keep him? As strong
as Merlyn's?'

What could I do but look down at her with the tears
beginning to brim in my eyes and hug her close to me.
She saw where the real danger lay.

When I lifted my head I thought I could hear a bell
on the wind and I pictured those little white figures
going to their chapel in the grey dawn light. Well,

what if they were? They'd be at their prayers now. I caught myself wondering if they were praying for us.

All the same I wasn't prepared for what I found later that morning. Morgan, with her hands lifted, praying out loud, and not to any god I'd sung to her of. She smiled when she saw my face, and then she looked frightened.

'What's the matter, Gwennol? Why are you looking so angry? Didn't you mean it? Haven't the Christians got the power to save us?'

'Them! No, my girl, they haven't,' I told her pretty short. 'So don't let me catch you looking to them to help you.'

I don't know to this day if I did right. I hadn't the power to save her myself, had I?

At sunrise we shut ourselves in the hall again. There was a ladder to the loft over our heads. Just in case. Elaine was weary and crying, but to Margawse it was all adventure. She'd enjoyed what we'd done last night. It was her first taste of our power, and it had quickened her blood. She was only sorry she couldn't be riding off to Dimiliock now to watch the battle. She hadn't the seeing, like Elaine.

Lady Ygerne sat with Elaine's head on her shoulder. She looked older by daylight. I wouldn't like to tell which way her hopes were turning. Morgan was quiet, too. She was more frightened, now that her father had left her.

Chapter Seventeen

We hadn't much longer to wait. When they came it was sudden, like a flood in February. Keby shouted out to us and we went running to the walls. I could hear our small old guard drawing their swords, grasping at spear and shield. But there was no hope of fighting.

I'd never seen such an army. I thought the hills themselves were moving. It was like the shadow of a great cloud in the east.

'They've taken his bait,' said Coan, very hoarse. 'They're bound for Dimiliock. They're going to pass us by.'

'Don't tempt the gods!' I screamed at him. But it was too late.

We watched the Pendragon's men pouring off the ridge towards us, like a river that has burst its banks, and spreading out over the countryside, in little rivulets. For a while the forest hid them. We could see smoke beginning to go up here and there. Then they were on us. Green and blue, their cloaks were, sweeping in to drown us where we stood. And the light on their weapons and harness flashing like water in the sun.

We weren't waiting out there in the open to see any more and be seen ourselves. We didn't need telling that the only safe place for us was up the ladder into the rafters over the great hall. Lady Ygerne and the three girls went first, with Gorlois's men after them. Their faces were grim and their swords were drawn, and not only for Uther Pendragon's soldiers, I knew.

Now Ruan and the slaves were scuttling up that ladder as fast as they could move. I told them all to go in front of me, for I knew I'd be the slowest. And all the time I was gabbling spells aloud that I'd forgotten I knew.

But when it came my turn to climb that ladder, my stiff old joints clipped at my sinews like the blacksmith's red-hot pincers. Morgan leaned over the hole, and her little white hand was clawing down for mine.

'Come on, Gwennol! Quickly!' she screamed.

There were many things happened that day that I wish I could forget, and can't. But I shall remember that one thing 'til the day I die. Morgan cried out for me as though she loved me.

But nothing I could do, not even the wet, shaking terror of the Pendragon's men, would get my limbs up those rungs. When they knew it was no good, old Sulian drew the ladder up into the shadows, and their faces disappeared.

That hall seemed bigger than I'd ever remembered it. Too big for me. But I daren't go outside again. So I crept into a corner behind the beer-pots. And then I thought that was the worst place I could have chosen to hide from soldiers, so I crawled away like a rat into another corner and hid myself in the straw. And only then I remembered Keby, that I'd last seen standing on the wall with nothing but an axe in his hand.

We couldn't know 'til the very last if they would pass us by or not. The coast road runs close by Bossiney. Surely they couldn't have helped but see our dun? I lay with my head pressed to the ground. I could feel my whole body shaking with the tramp of their feet and hear the neigh of their horses. They were coming fast, like hounds that have sighted their quarry. The sound was getting louder, like the tide coming in.

Then it seemed to go quiet and I thought we were saved. Maybe my spell-weaving had been stronger than I'd dared to hope. I lifted my face from that scratching straw. Too quick. There was a shout from outside. Then loud yelling. I dived back under that straw like an old trout under a stone. And there I lay, shivering with fright.

It didn't take them long. They burst through the door. I'd have given anything to be able to see with my ears then. I could hear shouting and banging, but I couldn't make sense of it. There didn't seem so many of them as I would have thought, and more of them inside the hall than out of it, by the sound of it. I could tell when they found the beer, and I thanked my lucky stars I wasn't behind it. Let them drink themselves stupid, I prayed. And I curled myself small like a new-born baby in a cold world.

But they found me. When they pulled the straw off me and rolled me over, they looked like a ring of giants with their backs to the light. Laughing down at me at the thought of what was coming as if I'd been thirty years younger. And they weren't drunk enough for my liking. It only made them rough. I tried to let them take me as easily as I could, for I was an old, used woman and long past the age of bearing, and what did it matter so long as it was over quickly? But I must have been stiff and difficult for all that. It was a long time since I'd had a man between my legs – except in the Mothers' service, and that is something different. Then there's that pulse in the blood that makes us all young maids again, wet inside and out and too eager for stopping, and the one who comes to us then takes us like a king. So they hurt me, and I cried out with the pain. But it was a cruel long time before they had all finished with me.

Someone else came then. A young warrior lord by the look of him, but he wasn't Uther. He was half-drunk as well. He shouted at the men, and they went grumbling out of the hall like whipped curs. But he stopped behind. It wasn't me he wanted. He looked all round and cursed. If he was hoping to find a treasure of weapons still hung on the walls, he could have saved himself the trouble. He might have known that Gorlois wouldn't leave so much as a horseshoe-nail behind for Uther Pendragon to find. So he had me like the rest before he left, since there wasn't anything better.

There wasn't one of them saw the treasure hidden over their heads. I never had Merlyn's power, and what I'd had felt to be slipping away from me fast, but I couldn't help having a grim sort of smile to myself, even then. That's one spell I'd made stronger than I'd thought.

He strode out of the door, and I heard him call for fire, and I thanked the gods that all our hearths were cold. But one of them must have had a flint. I heard it strike, and then a crackle in the thatch. I thought of my own skin first, even before Morgan's, crouching there as I was in that stale straw with the fire beginning to sparkle in the roof. And anyway, what had any of them done to help me? I'd done my best for them. Those that went up that ladder could get down it fast enough without help from me.

The noise died away. I limped out to the doorway and breathed clean air again. There was a dark cloud

of dust up on the ridge going away to the south. It
seemed King Uther had taken Gorlois's bait. But his
men had left Bossiney burning.

Well, let it burn. There wasn't water enough to put
it out. All I wanted was enough to wash myself clean.
I'd find some in the well behind the kitchen. I could
only go slowly and painfully. There was no one yet to
help me.

I pulled myself round the corner of the wall. And it
was there I found Keby, hanging over the well with
his throat cut like a pig.

A little voice spoke behind me. I might have known
Morgan would be quickest down that ladder.

'Is Keby dead? He is, isn't he? And those things they
did to you. Was that because of Mother, too?'

I was too sorry for myself to tell her anything but
the truth.

Chapter Eighteen

Bossiney burned. I hadn't the heart to weep for it. Sulian's three and the slaves did what they could to pull off the burning straw from the roofs with rakes and beat out whatever flames they could reach. But for all that, the great hall was a blackened shell, the stables had gone, and the slaves' quarters were nothing but smoke and ruin. They'd managed to save my lady's bower, though there was a great black hole in the roof. They'd all of them worked themselves to death there to salvage what they could. Even my lady and the girls had fought the flames and run through the smoke with whatever armfuls of stuff Uther's men might have missed. All except me, and I could hardly put one foot in front of another. They were all of them black and weary by the time they'd done.

Lady Ygerne pushed back her hair with her sooty hand and said, 'If Uther Pendragon could see me now, I doubt if he'd think I was worth the trouble of finding.'

And her voice trembled, so that I could tell she was near to tears. Poor lady. She hadn't had a mouthful of hot food for a night and a day, and she'd been frightened half out of her wits. But she was as proud as Gorlois, and that's where it hurt her most. She could bear it if her lord died in battle and King Uther took her by force. But what she couldn't bear was for him to come and find her like this, old and tired and dirty.

139

'There now,' I soothed her. 'We'll wash your pretty face and see if we can find you a clean gown, and there's still a corner to sleep in.'

'I won't stay here.'

'There's nowhere else for us, my handsome. We'll make shift somehow.'

'We can't spend another night waiting for common soldiers to come and burn us in our own thatch like rats,' said my lady.

'They won't come back. Not now they think the place is burned, and only a dead boy and an old used baggage like me inside.'

'And what are we to eat and drink?'

That made me pause a bit. I'd been bleating away at her like a foolish ewe, but I saw she had the better of me now. Sulian and Coan and Tudy had beaten back the flames from the storehouses, but they might as well have saved themselves the trouble. Bossiney was stripped bare: every last grain of corn and joint of salted pork gone. It was little enough Gorlois had left us to eat as it was, marching off with his own men at the thin end of winter with all the provisions they could carry for a siege. They'd even herded our cattle down the road to Dimiliock.

Siege? I couldn't see it, no matter how I tried. A proud man like Gorlois of Cornwall, waiting to die in his hole like a starved shrew, with Uther outside his gates, taunting him for the honour of his wife. A man like that would never stay cooped up for long.

But gone he was, and all our good corn with him, and what little he had left us, Uther's men had stolen.

And there was something worse. There wasn't one of us wanted to lift a bucket from that well, seeing what had fouled it. The men were old soldiers. They'd

140

seen blood before. But even they didn't have the stomach for that.

I didn't care then if I died, so long as I didn't have to move from where I was. All I wanted was somewhere to lay down my head and rest.

'We're to stay here. That was my lord's orders.'

'And how much longer will Duke Gorlois be alive to give anyone orders?'

'Ssh!' I scolded her, for Morgan was listening, with a face like white chalk under the soot. 'We'll face that news if it comes.'

'I won't stay here, like a pig shut in a slaughter-pen. It is not fitting.'

'But where would you go, my lover? You can't reach him now.'

She lifted her chin with that proud look that warned me I was not her nurse any more.

'Where we should always have gone. To the nuns at Tintagel.'

I looked to the warriors for help. They were Gorlois's men, after all, and under his orders. But I could see how it tempted them. They didn't like what they'd been told to do. And whatever Bryvyth said, even three old warriors might make a valiant stand there, defending my lady's honour on Tintagel causeway 'til the very last. You could watch the thought shaping in their minds.

'But my lord said . . .'

Ygerne looked me straight in the eye.

'Gorlois will not come back, Gwennol.'

I was too weary to argue with her.

I made the slaves get the better of themselves and dip the bucket in the well 'til they got one that was no worse than pink. You wouldn't have thought a young boy would have so much blood in him. But the Mothers

have more. They'll swallow all we give them 'til we're
bled white. But the water will still be bubbling up out
of the earth after we're gone.

Ruan chose a dark cloth and washed the soot from
their faces. There wasn't one of them dared to ask
where the water came from. And after they'd
finished, I cleaned my own legs with it. You can wish
to die, and yet you go on living.

But none of us cared to drink from that well, though
our throats were rasping from the smoke.

The men buried Keby in the meadow. Poor souls.
Their old arms were so weary they could hardly lift a
spade. But the pigs had been rooting for acorns under
the oaks all that wet winter, so the ground was soft. If
we lived, my lady would come back and ask Nectan to
give him a proper burial. The Church always had
them when they were dead.

Then those four wrapped themselves in their
cloaks, and put up their hoods to hide their faces. But
what was the good? You could no more have hidden
who they were than a white mare can hide in a herd of
bay and brown horses. Even the way they carried
their heads told they were nobly-born. The king would
find them out sooner or later. But Ygerne made sure
she would choose for herself the place where Uther
would see her again.

His men had gone long since. All the same, it was
queer and silent on the track. We all felt as naked as
babies as we stepped outside that gate. The pasture
was empty. There wasn't a body moving on the road.
Margawse was quieter than usual. She was looking
round her nervously instead of with that bold stare of
hers.

The cottages we passed had a dead sort of look.
Some of them had their doors wrenched off their

hinges and their gardens trampled and every bit of food gone. If they hadn't, the doors were shut, and the smoke-holes were still, as though the hearths below them were cold. They had an unfriendly feel. And with good reason. The bards sing fine songs of the warriors who fall in battle. But there are others the lays don't tell you of. There were common men as well as lords walled up in Dimiliock now who'd never come home again, and women and children who had cause to weep already. If they were inside, peeping at us through the cracks in the door as we passed by, they wouldn't have any reason to love Gorlois's family.

Elaine looked pale and scared, and kept close behind her mother and Sulian. Morgan was the bravest of the three, with her little head held high.

By the time we reached the cliffs, I was so worn out I couldn't look at more than the next step in front of me in the grass. Every time I moved a foot it hurt me. But when I had dragged myself out to the headland I drew a big breath and made myself lift my face to look south.

It was what I'd feared. The sky was filled with a great dust-fog, and I heard men screaming and the clash of weapons. But when I looked round at Sulian and his men I could tell by their faces they hadn't heard anything but the cry of herring-gulls and the splash of the breakers on the rocks beneath us. And they were soldiers that had known more battles than ever I would.

I'd have liked to believe they had the truth of it, and I was just a foolish old woman who'd seen too many horrors for one day. Then I looked at Elaine, and I knew she'd heard it too. It's a bitter burden we carry.

Morgan caught at my hand.

'How far is Dimiliock? Will we be able to see it from Tintagel?'

143

'No,' I said, to comfort her and myself. 'It's too far for the likes of you to see the fighting. Dimiliock's an hour's hard galloping from here.'

Still so close as that? They seemed to have been gone a lifetime.

'He should have taken me with him. I'm not afraid of the Pendragon. I'd have fought him. Like I fought the fire.'

'No, no,' I told her. 'You weren't made to be a warrior. You're forgetting. I thought you'd made up your mind to be a beautiful queen, like your mother.'

She pulled her hand away, sharpish-like. 'Don't dare say that! What made you do it, Gwennol? She's not a queen. Not while Father's alive. And anyway, I don't want to get married now. Not to a king or anyone else.'

And I didn't need to ask what she'd seen that day to make her change her mind.

There's a valley runs down below Tintagel. We came to the head of it, and there was the nunnery, standing against the sky like a fairy fortress. There was the cross on top, and little houses for the nuns all dotted around the sides. Peaceful, that's what it looked, like a farm in the evening when the cattle are coming home. Uther's men hadn't touched it.

They all of them started to hurry when they saw it. But I couldn't have gone any faster if I'd tried. Every step I took was agony, with the raw flesh chafing me as I moved my legs.

Morgan waited for me where the path crossed the stream and began to climb again. She smiled as she held out her hand and pulled me up. But then she was away again up to the next bend, darting backwards and forwards like a squirrel. She was always impatient.

144

I was far and away the last to reach the top. I couldn't help it. They were all standing there on the edge of the cliff, and I don't flatter myself it was me they were waiting for. An odd, quiet place, it was. Not a soul to be seen. There was a bank in front of us, with a narrow opening, to show that it was holy ground beyond. God's rampart, they called it.

And below it a deep ditch that must have taken days to dig. It made me feel queer looking down into it. But that was nothing to what I knew was waiting for us on the other side.

There was no one about. But for all that, I had a feeling we were being watched.

Chapter Nineteen

There was no one about, so we started to walk through. But we hadn't taken more than a few steps towards it before old Padern came out from behind his hut. From the way he was yawning I should say he'd been taking a nap in the sunshine, just as if Uther Pendragon's army wasn't raiding and burning the whole countryside. Well, they'd steered clear of Tintagel. There wasn't a wisp of burning thatch here.

His mouth fell open in a different way when he saw who'd come. Sulian gave him his marching orders.

'Bring your mistress here, fellow. And look sharp about it.'

He didn't need telling twice. He went hobbling away over the bridge as fast as he could go. Poor old man. I don't know what they kept him for. They were a tough lot, those nuns. Half of them were stronger than he was. But then, he was hardly likely to turn any woman's head.

While we waited we couldn't help looking at that neck of stone between us and the island. It wasn't very wide. I could hear the waves pounding on the rocks below, and it seemed to me as if each one that broke was biting a little bit deeper into the sides. I could almost fancy I felt the land shaking beneath me.

Padern was coming back. A little brown figure he

147

looked on that causeway, like a shrivelled old leaf
that the wind might blow away. He was fairly out of
breath by the time he got to us.

'You're to go across, my lady. She's waiting for
you.'

So Ygerne wasn't the only one who would have her
visitors meet her where she chose. I thought our
duchess might argue, but to tell you the truth, we'd had
enough of standing out there on the open downs. We'd
all feel a lot safer on the other side of that bridge.

So we kept our dignity and went on through the
gate. Ygerne first, then her daughters, with Ruan and
me following. But when it came to Sulian's turn
Padern stuck out his hand.

'I'm sorry, sir,' he said. 'Just the womenfolk unless
you give me your weapons. There's no armed men
allowed on Tintagel Island.'

Sulian had the sword half out of his scabbard. He
had his job to do. But Ygerne turned to him with a
sweet smile.

'Put up your sword, Sulian. I shan't need you to
defend me here.'

I felt sorry for those grey old warriors. They'd
rather have been at Dimiliock, any day. It was a hard
task my lord had left them. But they knew their duty.
They'd wait by the rampart if she ordered them. They
wouldn't budge from it, whoever came. And they
were not so old but they wouldn't sell their lives
dearly to anyone who tried to pass them.

My lady was walking out on to that high path, so we
had to follow her. It made me turn dizzy crossing that,
and I wouldn't be the first one, by a long way. You
could look down into the sea on both sides, ten times
deeper than the deepest well. Green water breaking
on black stone. And you could see where lumps of

148

rock had tumbled off and lay smashed on the beach, like bits of broken pot. Up here in the sunshine it might be all peaceful and holy to Christ. But underneath there was something else. A different holiness, where the two streams meet. The Mother's Hole. The nuns should have known they'd never be rid of it entirely.

I wondered then if my lady had more than I guessed in mind when she chose this place. There was power beneath us. I could feel it with every step. What troubled me was what she meant to use it for.

I looked down at Morgan. But for once her little face was hidden under her hood.

There was a nun waiting to meet us on the other side. But she was too small to be Bryvyth. She wore white wool that had never been dyed, the same as they all did, and walked bare-footed. But she greeted us like a lady in her own hall.

'The peace of Christ welcomes you,' she called out to us, 'and the rest of the Spirit upon weary travellers.'

'May your peace return to you,' we answered, as they had taught us.

Peace? Small hope of that, I thought to myself, what with the pain in my guts and the thought of Keby with his blood running away into the well, and Uther Pendragon laying Cornwall waste, all for the sake of my lady's face.

Well, as for her, she held her head so high she might have been visiting another lady in her castle for a feast. 'Lady Ygerne and the three daughters of Gorlois claim sanctuary here from Uther Pendragon.'

That made the little nun gasp.

'Follow me!' she said.

She was off up the path with her skirt flapping, like a startled hare. All over the island we could see white

149

figures turning round or peering out of doorways to get a good look at us.

'That's made a stick to stir the hive,' I muttered to Ruan.

The little nun showed us into the guest-house.

'Wait here,' she said, 'Bryvyth is coming herself.' And she bobbed away backwards out of the door.

I'd never been inside a convent before. Seeing those plain, white nuns, I'd always thought they must live in a poor, bare place. But whatever their own cells were like, when I looked around their guest-house they had tables and benches as finely made as anything we'd had in Bossiney before it was burned. And the curtain that hung by the door was made of wool good enough for a chieftain's cloak.

But I hadn't much time to be nosy. Next thing we knew, there was Bryvyth in the doorway. A big, broad-shouldered woman she was, and she stood on her own threshold like a barn-door. I thought for a moment her knee began to bend when she saw us, as if she was going to bow to Lady Ygerne. But if she had old habits pulling her that way, she got the better of them.

'Peace be to all in this house, and the blessed rest of angels this night,' she said.

'And to you also,' we answered.

'And which of you would be the Lady Ygerne?'

They still had their hoods on. But she knew, of course. Hadn't her own hands given the wine to my lady that very Sunday? You couldn't have hidden a fine duchess like Ygerne among a hundred women. And anyway, Bryvyth was looking straight at her when she said it. But she was mistress in her own house, bare feet or not, and she was enjoying it.

My lady drew herself up tall. For all she had come

through, she looked as fine and handsome in her
homespun cloak as if it had been cloth of gold.

'I am the duchess,' she said. 'My lord Gorlois is
fighting with Uther Pendragon at Dimiliock, and I and
my daughters have had our hall burnt down about our
ears by his soldiers. We claim sanctuary here, with
you, for our lives and honour.'

I thought that nun looked at her shrewdly.

'And you're thinking Uther Pendragon would
respect my convent, now? What's to stop him going
through here like a blacksmith's poker through
butter?'

'Uther is a Christian king.'

'A fine sort of Christian, isn't it, that makes war on
the husband to steal his wife?'

'He is High King of all the Britons. He is used to
having what he wants.'

'For a king so recently made, it's not taken him long
to get into the habit. And if you've come from his feast
in London, you'll know it's no Christian confessor he
keeps company with for his soul-friend.'

There was not much she hadn't heard, that
Bryvyth. And she was sharper than Nectan.

'Is it Merlyn you speak of?' my lady asked, and I
thought she spoke the name soft and carefully.

'Emrys Merlyn it is. And no friend of the Church.'

I waited for my lady to answer that. When she did
she startled me.

'Uther Pendragon carries the cross into battle.
Whoever helps him fights for you, Bryvyth Crook-
Staff.'

'And if he wins, who will be master on Tintagel
tomorrow? My Lord, or Merlyn's?'

'If the Saxons win, there will be no tomorrow for
either of you.'

151

The nun snorted and straightened her shoulders then, like a farmer's wife getting ready to draw a pig.

'Well, they'll not be coming tonight, by the look of it. We'll see what the morning brings. There are clean beds here for the women, if that will suit you. Padern will look to your men in the gatehouse. So I'll see you at supper. We don't get many guests at Tintagel. It's a long time since I had a crack with layfolk that could talk about more than the price of beans.'

She looked across the bridge at the porter's lodge.

'And send word to those men of yours that they can put their swords away and sleep sound tonight. This is a holy place. If Uther Pendragon should come to Tintagel, it's me he will have to reckon with.'

She left us then with a grim smile. The guest-mistress brought warm water and washed our feet, even mine. It was sweet to the touch, that pure spring water. It cleaned more than our skin. And when we drank it cold it tasted better than wine.

The sun was getting low, though we couldn't see it now. A mist was creeping in and the tide was hushed. Presently a bell rang and we could hear the nuns singing in the chapel higher above us. Away in Dimiliock, the first day's fighting would be nearly over. It was a heavy thought that there'd be men dead now that I'd known all their lives. And nothing any of us could do but wait.

They served us a fine supper in their refectory. It opened my eyes, I can tell you. Red wine in glass goblets, just for the gentry, of course. And roast lamb, newly-killed, on fine, glazed dishes. Bryvyth laughed at our faces.

'Yes. We lead a simple life most of the year. But it's our rule to see our pilgrims well-served. Guests are doubly welcome!'

152

And when I looked at the nuns I could see what she meant. They were sat at tables down the sides, and they were enjoying their feast, I can tell you. Across the bottom of the room there were the schoolgirls. Princesses as well as farmers' daughters, so I'd heard. They weren't allowed to talk, but they were staring at us for all they were worth.

The wine loosed Bryvyth's tongue, and she was all evening telling Ygerne about her schooling in Dyfed. Of how she'd travelled in Ireland, following him she called Patrick. And of the work of her nuns that were fine potters and weavers and bee-keepers and scribes, and were supposed to busy themselves with everything that was wholesome and beautiful.

Pilgrimage, that's what she called her life. A journey of the soul. Always travelling on to something new.

More than once her eyes went to my face. But she never challenged me. And I was too weary to think it strange for me to be sitting at her table. It was like a dream to us at the end of such a day to be full and warm and at ease, and to feel the arms of the sea guarding us on every side but one. It ended with Elaine asleep with her head on the table, and Morgan creeping into my arms to close her eyes.

We got them to bed at last. The guest-house had three small rooms, opening off a passageway. My lady slept in the far one, with Ruan stretched at her feet. Elaine and Margawse next to them, and I was left with Morgan. We were too tired out and full of food and wine to fear that anyone might come on us in the dark. We didn't trouble ourselves how Coan and Tudy and Sulian might be passing the night on the other side of the bridge.

I shuffled in to put the older girls to bed, and I'd

hardly the strength to brush their hair or fold their gowns. We should none of us want rocking that night, after all we'd been through. I'd be gladder than most to close my eyes and put the pain away.

When I got back to Morgan she was standing in her shift at the open window, watching the mist come creeping up over the cliffs and curling in wisps in front of her eyes. She had her back turned to me, and her voice sounded hollow in the fog.

'Where are we? What place is this?'

'Why, maid, you know very well where we've come. To the nunnery at Tintagel, as your mother said.'

After a bit she swung round to me, her eyes black and staring.

'Who are you? Who am I?'

That made me shiver, I can tell you, thinking of some of those charms I had put about us. How did I know what she could see or couldn't see when she looked at me? It made me cross and frightened.

'Hold your tongue now, child, and come to bed. Do you want to ill-wish us all? I'm old Gwennol, and you're little Morgan, that's Lord Gorlois's daughter.'

'Am I? Am I, old woman?'

I couldn't bear to listen to such nonsense any longer, nor meet the look in her eyes. I rolled over, hunched up tight under my blankets, and tried to wish that long day away. Beneath us I could hear the slow beat of the sea. Like the breath of a living beast, it was, closer than I had ever slept to it before. I knew the tide was rising in the Mother's Hole. And even there in the darkness, with my eyes tight shut, I had a picture of Morgan still, kneeling on her bed in her white shift, staring at me as though she didn't know me.

Chapter Twenty

I woke suddenly in the night, with that feeling you have when you know there's something wrong. I sat up in bed, and that made me draw my breath sharp. My scars had stiffened while I slept and the crust was splitting. I listened. I couldn't hear a sound now. And somehow that was worse than if I had. I waited, with the skin crawling on my neck, and then I heard it. A scratching on a door, and then a bumping in the passage, and the sound of men's voices, very low.

I'd no thought but that Uther's men were coming to attack us in our beds. Then I heard women whispering. And I thought perhaps they might still be outside the gate and old Padern had come across the bridge in the dark to warn Lady Ygerne. And what could we do if he had? We'd nowhere left to run.

I clambered out of bed, and I don't mind telling you it made me moan to move. I went to the chamber-door and I must have gasped out loud, for there was a white-clad figure whisking out of the house-door into the night. I made the sign against evil. Then I blinked and came to my senses a bit, for as she vanished over the step I saw the heel of her bare foot and knew it must have been one of Bryvyth's nuns. The little guest-mistress probably. She'd left the outer door open, but I couldn't see far. The moon was up, but so was the mist. The air was white, yet I could hardly see

two paces beyond the step. It was a night to trick the
eyes. Far below I could just about hear the hiss of the
sea. Even that had gone quiet now, as if it was listening.

I put a bar of my own kind on that door, just to be
sure, mumbling a bit, as you do when you're not really
thinking. And I cursed myself for an old fool that had
broken a good night's rest for nothing, and got the cold
dew on me. Then I turned back, and I had such a shock!
It sent the blood out of my face all at once when I saw
what I'd done. If my bar had worked, it had shut the
good outside and trapped the evil in with us.

Two men were standing on either side of my lady's
chamber-door, like sentries. Tall men, cloaked and
hooded. They were none of our three old veterans, that
we'd left at the gate, for they carried themselves
straight and easy, like warriors in the prime of life.
I couldn't move for fear, and my tongue stuck in my
throat.

I knew they were watching me, though they had
shadows for eyes. Then they turned their heads to look
at each other and I heard them laugh low.

Well, if I'd been afraid to venture outside my room,
first off, it was worse now. I was trembling like a dog in
a thunderstorm. I'd have given a year of my life to be
back in bed with the covers over my head. But I daren't
step past those two men and turn my back on them,
even if they'd let me by. Then another shape separated
itself from the shadows between those soldiers. A
woman's, it was.

'Ruan?' I gasped, with my heart in my mouth. It's not
often I've been glad to see her, but I couldn't think who
else it could be.

It was her, all right, and she giggled to me, with a
bright, wicked look in her eyes, that put me in mind of
Margawse.

'Ssh!' she whispered. 'What's the matter? Don't
you recognise these two? It's Jordan and Britael.'

My lord's two bodyguards, that hardly left his side?
I couldn't make sense of it. Or only one way.

'Is he dead, then?'

'No! You ninny, Gwennol! Lord Gorlois is here. He's
in my lady's room now.'

'He never is!'

'It's true. He'll be having her in her bed by now.'

'But he's in Caer Dimiliock, with the Pendragon's
army round him. How could he get out?'

There was a movement from the middle room behind
us, where Elaine and Margawse slept. I heard Elaine
cry out.

'No! No!'

And then Margawse hushing her.

'Ssh. Don't disturb the children.' Ruan put her finger to her lips. 'What does it matter how he did it?
Let's leave my lord and lady in peace. They'll sleep
sweet tonight. If they sleep at all!'

I looked past her. Those two tall guards had never
moved, nor lifted the hoods back from their faces. But
I could see their white teeth grinning in the shadows.

One of them murmured, 'Goodnight, Gwennol.' It
was Jordan's voice, all right.

I breathed a little easier. To tell you the truth, I
wanted to believe her. I'd had enough terror to last
me a lifetime. I'd known those two since my Ygerne
had married Gorlois. A wild-spirited pair they'd been
then, like Gorlois himself. That was the sort of hare-
brained trick those three would have played, to steal
out of a fort under siege, past the very nose of the king
himself. Like schoolboys scrumping. And our Cornish
orchards grow a rosy apple.

And then the smile slipped from my face. He was

Duke of Cornwall, wasn't he? And Ygerne was his own wife. He shouldn't need to steal in to her like a thief in the night.

I shook my head and closed the chamber-door behind me. I couldn't understand a word of it. I'd been so sure we'd never see Lord Gorlois alive again. One Cornish lord against all the hosts of Britain? Besides, I knew his temper. If Gorlois couldn't win, he'd never run away. He'd chosen to take his stand at Caer Dimiliock, and he'd die fighting there. And who could have told him he'd find us in Tintagel?

Tintagel! Gorlois, to beg his way in past Bryvyth?

It wasn't exactly a sound I heard behind me. More like a chill stir in the air, as though someone had unbarred the window. But I knew, even in the darkness, what it was. Morgan was awake and listening.

'What is it? What did she say?'

'Hush, my lover. It's nothing. Go back to sleep.'

'No. Tell me. She said something about Father, didn't she? Is he dead?' She screeched it out at me. 'He is, isn't he? Is that what they've come to say?'

I went to her, and felt for her shoulders in the darkness. She clung to me like a wild thing, and I stroked her hair.

'No, my pretty. It's not that.' And then it came out in a rush, to comfort her. 'Your father's alive. He's here. He's come to your mother.'

I should have known better. She was out of my arms, and what chance had I got of holding her?

Then she screamed, outside in the passage. And hurt or not, I was out of that door faster than you'd have thought possible.

I couldn't see her at first. But I saw someone else. In a patch of moonlight, from the door. Not Ruan, this time. Oh, no, not Ruan. The other of those men had

moved. Taller than any warrior I'd ever seen, or so he
looked then. Standing in a shaft of gossamer light,
brighter than mist and thicker than moonshine. With
a hood drawn over his face, shadowing it. Then I
made out that he had Morgan by the wrists and she
was fighting him like a wildcat.

'Let me go! Let me go! I want to see my father!'

Then the hood fell back as he struggled to hold
Morgan. I breathed a sigh of relief. I'd been having
nightmares with my eyes open for nothing. His face
was half-lit in the witchlight, but it was the one I
knew: Britael's, that had been my lord's bodyguard
these fifteen years, and his friend before that.

'Take your claws out of me, you little screech-owl,
or by the hounds of Annwn, I'll put that on you that
will bind you stiller than stone from now till morning.'

He had a deep, strong voice, like wind through the
standing stones, but this time my knees fairly shook
when I heard it. I wasn't a fool. I knew every man in
Gorlois's dun. The voice was Britael's, I didn't doubt
that. But Britael would never in his life have spoken
words like those. I could only think of one man who
would.

But Morgan didn't care who he was. She ducked
her face to his hand and he let out a yell. And from the
bedroom behind him there came another shriek. A
woman's cry, that stopped us all in our tracks. To this
day I couldn't tell you if it was joy or pain, or both at
once. But as long as I live I shall still hear that cry. It
was as if the land itself had been entered.

That voice that was Britael's laughed long and
loud.

I snatched Morgan to me and covered her ears with
my arms. None of us should have heard what we had.
Inside my head I could hear my own voice crying out,

'Where are our guards? Sulian! Oh, Mother, where are the guards?' When I listened again there was only the splash of the waves below us, and I knew I hadn't spoken a word. All I saw was what seemed to be Britael's face, smiling at me from the shadows, and the shape like Jordan's grinning at me too. There wasn't a sword in the world could have saved us from those smiles then.

Morgan was flying at him again, but that tall man threw her across the passage, as a wolf might toss a whippet over a stream.

'The little weasel! She bit me. Get her to bed, woman, 'til tomorrow. And look to it well that she doesn't trouble her mother again.'

I could hear Elaine weeping behind the wall, and Margawse whispering. But I hadn't a thought for either of them.

Morgan was sobbing now.

'Father! Where is Father?'

'Hush, my pretty,' I told her, dragging her back into our chamber. 'Your father is sleeping now. Sound and long. We shall all of us go to join him soon enough.'

Chapter Twenty-one

Somehow I slept again, and as heavily as if I'd been drugged. When I woke it was full morning. Morgan was sitting at the open window, with the sea-wind slapping the hair across her face like a whiplash. The mist had gone and the breeze was skimming up the crests off the waves like flags.

I looked at the door, and though I knew it was foolishness, I was afraid to step out into that passage. I knew he wasn't there but the terror of it was still on me. You'll think me a silly old fool, crying my eyes out one day because I hadn't met him, and shaking with fear the next because I had. But you haven't known him. I'm not talking about an ordinary man.

Morgan turned her head slowly to look at me, with a strange, cold stare.

'You needn't be afraid. I heard them go.'

And there was a queer thing for her to say, when she'd been so hot to see her father last night. Hadn't she so much as opened the door to see if I was telling her the truth? My mouth fell open, but I didn't know what to say to her. There was a bleak, shut look in her face that I had never seen before. I didn't like it. She'd always worn her heart naked in her eyes.

'See for yourself,' she said, very cool and scornful, not like her tempers or her wheedling smile.

I went to the door, stiff and slowly. But I knew she

161

was right. The passage was empty. There was no sign of any men.

The bell was ringing the nuns to their chapel.

I don't know what I was afraid of finding out, but I didn't go to my lady's room straight off. I stopped at the older girls' door and poked my head in. Elaine was fast asleep, curled up like a plump, round dormouse for comfort. There were tear-marks on her face, and she was sighing in her sleep. But Margawse was sitting up with the covers thrown back and her shift open to her breasts. There was a funny, wild look about her.

'Is he come yet. Gwennol? Has Uther Pendragon found us? We thought we heard voices in the night, but we daren't look. Listen! Isn't that the gallop of horsemen coming?'

'Never you fear, now. It's only the sea on the rocks. You're safe here,' I said, helping her to dress.

It wasn't like Margawse to be frightened. She wasn't the only one. I had a cold feeling that something had happened here that was too late to mend.

I went back to dress myself, and Morgan too. Then I straightened my shoulders and tried to act braver than I felt. Even then I daren't have told you what I feared. I tiptoed to the end of the passage, to my lady's room, and scratched at the door. When I opened it, Ruan was lying at the foot of the bed. Her eyes were open, watching me. She put her fingers to her lips.

Ygerne was asleep, in that narrow convent bed, with her face turned towards me. She hardly looked any older than Elaine. But there were no tears on her cheeks. She was smiling in her sleep. And far be it from me to speak ill of my betters, but when I saw her lying there like that I could have slapped her face.

What right had she to look so pink and pretty, when the rest of us were as white as whey?

Whole, she looked, when the rest of us were wounded. Full and satisfied, when her daughters had been robbed. I knew what that look meant well enough.

I went outside to cool my temper in the good sea-wind. It seemed quiet enough in the sunshine, though the waves were roaring on the beach. I could believe Margawse's fancy, that it was like a great troop of horsemen galloping nearer. All over the island I could see the nuns busy at their work. And it seemed to me that their movements were brisker than the day before. I've seen birds darting here and there like that when their nest is threatened. Two were herding the cows out from milking, and some were sitting out of doors, seemingly writing. It was strange to me to see those women with pens in their hands. Their houses were not like the buildings of a dun, all tight together inside a wall. They were scattered about the grass, with their doors open to the sea and the wind, as though those nuns didn't mind being alone with their thoughts. But they were lifting their heads pretty often to look at the bridge.

As I watched, there was a bit of a flurry among them, like wind passing over a field of corn before a storm. I turned just in time to see Bryvyth striding up the path towards the guest-house.

'Bring the Lady Ygerne outside to speak to me!'

A fine, commanding voice she had, that nun.

From inside, I heard Ruan's voice call out.

'My lady is sleeping. Tell her to wait.'

But Bryvyth was not a woman to be kept waiting.

'Lady Ygerne! Come out!' She thundered.

There was a silence. And then Ygerne stood in the

doorway, with a white and gold gown we'd rescued from the fire slipped hastily on and her pretty hair unbraided. Her chin was up, but she looked younger than ever.

'Come here!' the nun bellows.

The rest were all creeping up to watch. Bryvyth stood on the path with her nuns gathered behind her, like a stag guarding its does.

'Kneel!'

Ygerne's mouth opened then, and I thought she would say no to that. There was a mighty long moment of awful silence. Then she smiled, and down she went, Gorlois's lady on the muddy grass in her fine gown. And it was so quiet you could hear the sea sliding down between the stones, like horses whinnying. I've often wondered how much she was laughing at all of us.

The nun wasn't laughing.

'The holy gate of Tintagel was opened last night, after dark. They told me Lord Gorlois had come with two companions, in danger of their lives, to see his wife. For Christian pity I broke our rule. I had the gate unbarred and let them in. Armed men entered this holy island, the Blessed Virgin forgive me! As you value your soul, answer me. Was it your lord who came to you? Did you take him to your bed, here?'

'Yes.' No more than a meek whisper, it was.

'Yet now it is morning and what was done in the darkness is made plain. Uther Pendragon's herald is at our gates. Lord Gorlois is dead. Woman, your husband fell last night at sunset, fighting against the king at Dimiliock. He died of his wounds. And Uther Pendragon has come to claim his wife.'

Well, I'd been watching Ygerne pretty close but it was only a moment I saw it – that flash of lightning in her eyes.

Then I spun round fast enough like all the rest. And what a sight met our eyes! Beyond the causeway was a great troop of horsemen drawn up on the hill facing us. The sun was bright on their weapons and shields and armour and the brave colours of their cloaks. They sat still on their horses with their heads high, waiting as bold as brass, and every so often a horse threw up its neck and whinnied. It wasn't a raiding-party this time. There wasn't a sword drawn. He'd won. You could tell even from here there was a grin on all their faces. Oh, no, the Pendragon hadn't come here to fight for Ygerne. He had come to claim what was his own already.

Then Ygerne flashed out at Bryvyth, with her sweet little chin in the air.

'Fool! Look! Can you not see it is Uther Pendragon's spears that keep you Christians safe? Where do you suppose the Church will be if the white dragon comes west?'

'Where it began! Under a tyrant. Did you think the Lamb was a stranger to the knife? The road runs straight from Gethsemane to here.'

Big Bryvyth folded her arms. You'd have thought she wasn't afraid of a Saxon army, or a British one either.

'Go! To your king, and his banners, and his spearmen. Adulteress! Did you imagine we needed your sin to shield *this*?'

Ygerne changed colour then. She went a deep fox-glove red. Not just her face, but down her neck and her breast. If she'd been a slug across the path, I think Bryvyth would have looked at her more kindly.

The nun wiped her hands then, as if she'd been gutting mackerel. I've a notion she was enjoying herself now.

165

'Go!' she thundered. 'Go to that godless man! And never set foot on this holy ground again unless you come with your hair shorn and your clothes rent to do penance for your blasphemy.'

We were dismissed from Tintagel. Tipped off their land. The land that had once been ours. I could feel the earth beginning to burn under the soles of my feet.

There was nothing else Ygerne could do, except keep her dignity. She got to her feet without a word and started down the path. The nuns stepped away into the grass to let her pass, and pulled their skirts aside. That family would never be right with the Church again.

But there was one they forgot. I don't know if the nuns could have healed her even then, but Bryvyth never thought of it. It cost her dearly afterwards. She lost the place that was dearest to her heart, not to the Saxons but through a slip of a girl barely come to womanhood.

I was as bad as the rest.

We'd none of us noticed there was something else between Ygerne and the Pendragon. A tiny black figure out on the bridge of stone. Morgan. Alone on that causeway. Facing a whole army. With the wind tearing her hair backwards like a raven's wing.

Chapter Twenty-Two

Ygerne stopped. It wasn't the drop to the sea she was afraid of, but her own daughter, staring at the Pendragon's army as though she could kill them with her fierce green eyes.

It was a fearsome place, that causeway. No walls on either side, not even a handrail. And the breakers so far below it made you giddy to look, smashing themselves on those rocks, one after the other, 'til the end of time.

We all seemed to stand there bewitched, nuns, warriors, king, lady, as if she'd put a spell on us. Then I straightened my shoulders. After all, she was my little maid. I'd carried her in my heart these eight years. And likely enough she was the last child that would ever be put in my lap to nurse. If her own mother couldn't go to her across that gulf that separated them – and it was more than sea-wind and gusty air – then I would, who had lived closer to her than her own blood.

There wasn't one of them tried to stop me. I walked past my lady, who was stopped as still as a standing stone, and down to that road of rock. The king was riding slowly down the slope on the other side. I knew it must be him, with his two tall warriors on either side. I wouldn't let myself look at them.

I'd seen Morgan tense. She was as still as a

thin-backed stoat, rearing up in the grass when it sees its prey. And near nine years though I'd known her, I'd no notion what she might do next.

I was afeared of them all. That drop to the waves, the king and his soul-friend smiling beside him, that had tricked us, the hundreds of swords in front, and that big nun behind. And most of all, if you'll believe me, that fatherless child no higher than my own chest.

I thought I'd call to her as I stepped out on the bridge. But my tongue was dry, and the wind snatched the breath out of my mouth. The pounding of those waves seemed to crash through my head and drove all the sense away. And yet it felt so quiet where we were. Just the two of us in a world of our own, high up there in the blue air. My old feet shuffling without a sound over the soft turf towards her. Her back was turned to me. All this time she never stirred a muscle. I could only guess what she was going to do. The only bit of her that moved was her black hair streaming out past her shoulders in the wind.

At last I found my voice, when I was hardly an arm's length from her. And very gruff and sudden it must have sounded, fool that I was.

'Come here, my lover. Come to Gwennol. There's nothing you can do will bring your father back to us now.'

I saw her start, just as the stoat jumps in the air. And she was whirling round and flying at me, teeth bared and nails clawing. I stumbled backwards and lost my balance. I heard men's voices shouting and women's screaming, and I don't doubt my own scream was somewhere there amongst all the rest. I saw the blue sky wheeling past me, and then the flash

of the sea on the horizon. There was silver, then
emerald green, spinning closer underneath me, purple
weed, white surf, black rock, and I was falling towards
it. Something caught me at the last. I felt the jolt
through all my bones as I went pitching over the edge.
I heard the sound of cloth tearing and I knew I was
going again.

Then her hands gripped me hard. She hauled me
back from the brink and staggered on to the path with
me. I was sobbing and panting like a woman in labour.
But Morgan flung her little bony arms around me and
buried her head in my breast, weeping fit to break her
heart.

We clung to each other, so close you couldn't have
separated us. She sobbed, 'I'm sorry, Gwennol! I'm
sorry!' And I just stroked her tangled hair and gasped
her name, over and over, as though I had lost my wits.
And for all the terror of it, I have wished often and
often that I could have that morning again. That was
the last time Morgan, Lord Gorlois's daughter,
hugged me and cried in my arms.

Then she twisted apart from me and turned away.
When she faced me again she was a different person.
It was as though she had gone from me further than I
could ever reach. Her face was hard and cold as
stone. I knew then I had lost her for sure.

My fall had broken her spell. On the far side of the
bridge the king's voice called, 'Ygerne!' I looked up at
Uther Pendragon then for the first time. Tall, he was,
and he sat proudly on his horse, for all a little maid
had just stopped him in his path. The warrior on his
right hand wore his cloak tossed over his shoulder
now, and his armour twinkled in the sun. He watched
us all with a crooked smile. I didn't swoon over Emrys
Merlyn this time. I stood my ground between Tintagel

and all the men and faced him back. Even in the morning sunlight, with his hood thrown back, he had still a little of the look of Britael about him. But not enough for me to forgive him what he'd done.

When Ygerne heard Uther Pendragon calling to her, she seemed to come to her senses and remember who she was. She turned her back on those Christian nuns she'd knelt in front of, and lifted her head and smiled at him. Then she walked across that bridge of stone, straight past her daughter Morgan, as though she couldn't see her.

Widowed that very day she may have been. But in her white gown, with her hair loose on her shoulders, she only needed a wreath of flowers round her head, and she would have looked for all the world like a May Queen.

Chapter Twenty-Three

You may think by now that I hated Uther Pendragon.
But that was before I knew him.

When my lady went out of Tintagel to go to him,
there was nothing the rest of us could do but follow
her, though Morgan hung back at the last. We passed
the porter's lodge and went through the gate in the
rampart, and suddenly Ygerne seemed to move as if
she felt she was free. She almost ran to Uther.

And he sat on his horse, like the high king that he
was, watching Gorlois's wife come to him, with a
great, satisfied smile on his face. And a tall friend on
either side of him.

As she passed Merlyn, she turned her face to him
for a moment and their eyes met. They smiled at each
other. Short and polite, it was, like two swordsmen
meeting, searching out each other's strengths and
weak points. I stopped short when I saw that and it
made me shiver. For wasn't she Ygerne, that I'd
nursed on my knee when she was still soiling her nap-
kins? And hadn't I taught her all the wisdom that she
knew? But there was a good deal more that I could
have told her I'd kept to myself. So, duchess or no,
who was she, that she could smile so boldly back at
Emrys Merlyn, when I daren't? What had she got
more then me, wise as I was, save a pretty face and a
womb that could still bleed?

Then Uther sprang down from his horse to greet her as though she was already his queen. But now that she'd got him, she wasn't going to have him seem less than he was, in front of all those people. She sank down on the grass in front of him, with a great billowing curtsy, and bowed her head. She had beautiful hair, had Ygerne, thick and golden, and with her face hidden you couldn't have seen those first wrinkles in the corners of her eyes.

He raised her up, of course. Not daintily, either. It was like a great bear-hug, and they kissed each other as warmly as if they'd been man and wife. I daren't look at Morgan's face.

He had chariots waiting. Very sure of himself was Uther Pendragon. He never doubted that he could take what he wanted, even from the holy house of a nunnery. He lifted Ygerne into one, as if she had been an armful of swansdown. Then he turned to the two older girls and took Elaine by the waist.

She was crying now for her father, and for fear of the soldiers, I don't doubt, and all the sudden terror and strangeness we'd had these two days. He put his arms round her and held her close to him, and he whispered in her ear for a little while. When she lifted her head from his shoulder she smiled up at him and started to dry her eyes.

As for Margawse, I needn't tell you the look that passed between them when his arms reached out to take her. It's not for me to say if that one wept for her father. But she knew very well how tears could put a sparkle in her eyes. He wouldn't be the first she'd flashed her dewdrops at, by a long way. And never a red eyelid or a puffy cheek on her. Not like Elaine, that seemed to be the only soft-hearted one of them, though I've sometimes wondered if she was all she seemed. When he swung Margawse up into the chariot after her sister, they were a mighty long time separating his cloak-pin from the breast of her gown, and there were roses in her cheeks by the time he'd finished.

Then he turned to Morgan, but she twisted her face away from him. And his eyes met mine across her head. Bright brown eyes, he had, and laughing for joy because he'd got what he wanted. And, may the Mothers give me peace, I almost forgave him. I was an old woman, older by far than my lady, and I'd had many men. But that was all it took. One smile from Uther Pendragon. And if he could make me feel like that after all he'd done to me and those I loved, it was time I started thinking less hardly of Ygerne.

But Morgan wouldn't let his hands touch her. She sprang up into the chariot all by herself, and if she could have made those horses rear up and strike their hooves in Uther's face, you could tell by the look in her eyes that she'd have done it.

I'd dearly loved to have ridden pillion behind one of the men, the way I was feeling. But you don't expect the gentry to notice things like that. They'd all forgotten me. So they moved off, all those fine riders with their spears held high and their gay cloaks blowing in the wind and the horns sounding, and Ygerne in her chariot at the front. I was left to walk behind. And my parts were still sore.

I looked round for some sign of Sulian and the other two. But I never saw them again after that. Or Jordan and Britael. There'd be more than a few women weeping around Bossiney after that night's work, and many a week before Nectan and his like had finished singing litanies for the dead.

I trudged along the track choked with their dust.

173

Then I heard horse's hooves coming up beside me. A pure white mare. That startled me, as you can guess. What Cornishman would have dared put a leg over her? No ordinary one, anyway. We've been the people of Rhiannon's horse as long as anyone knows. So I didn't need to look further.

Well, it's one thing to be warned, but another thing to build a wall in the time you've got. That tall, lean man was close above me in his skirt of mail and his green mantle with the hood thrown back on his shoulders. A proper warrior he looked this morning. Nothing druid about him now, except for the mare. But for all he was smiling, I could see close up that his face was lined deep, as if he'd seen more blood and heard more screams than a man so young could bear lightly. So I knew he had the seeing too. And I pitied him, whatever he'd done.

He was looking down at me with green-grey eyes that went clean through my head and out the other side. It was not like the way King Uther smiled at a woman. But it set my blood beating like the drums on May-morning, I can tell you.

'Gwennol,' he said, very low and courteous. 'Gwennol Far-Sight, is it? Do you know who I am, this morning?'

That brought me back. I don't know how I dared, but I looked him straight in the face.

'Merlyn, I should call you, sir. This morning.'

'Merlyn, it is. So it seems there is more than one wise woman in Cornwall.'

And what did he mean by that, I wonder? There were many of us in Cornwall, but few higher than me.

'There are some that say so.'

'Then we should be allies, you and I. I serve the king and you the queen.'

174

'She's not queen yet.' It came out so sharp it might have been Morgan's voice speaking through my lips.

'But will be soon, when Gorlois is buried. And she is still your mistress. By daylight at least.'

'It was Lord Gorlois gave me my meat these fifteen years.'

I saw his hands tighten on the bridle, and I had a hard job not to flinch.

'Then listen, Gwennol Far-Sight. Listen to me well, if you have any love for Gorlois's youngest daughter. That's a wild young hawk you have in your nest. See to it that she keeps her talons away from the king's flock. He's a man that likes to have nothing stand in his way.'

I was too full to speak. I couldn't answer him. Couldn't any of those grinning red dragons understand what they'd done to my little maid? But for all that, when he spoke so grave, I was all of a tremble, and I couldn't look him in the eye any more. He saw too much.

Then all of a sudden he laughed. And before I could let out a gasp, he'd got me by the waist and swung me up on the horse behind him. And I had to cling on tight as we galloped back to the army. Me, Gwennol Far-Sight, on the white mare that should have run free without a bridle, with my arms round the greatest druid in all Britain. The Mothers forgive me, I think I was laughing.

I soon saw that it hadn't taken some others long to forget to cry, either. There was the king on his horse beside Margawse and Elaine's chariot, and teasing and laughing with them both. It was that plump little hen, Elaine, that surprised me. Giving him back jest for jest she was, as if she'd forgotten she'd ever been shy. Forgotten too that he'd just killed her father, and then done worse than that.

I'd never seen Elaine quicken to a man before. It was like seeing her come awake from a long sleep. All her life she'd been one for mothering things, kittens and dolls and such. And here was Uther Pendragon teaching her that if she wanted to be a mother she'd have to learn to be a woman first. And he was a man that taught that very well.

But Morgan was only a child with a flat chest, scowling at him. He hardly looked at her twice. He'd forgotten already how she'd made him check at the bridge. Only Merlyn would remember that. You couldn't fool those eyes. I knew that he'd seen that last change in her face as well as I had. He knew what it meant. There was one at least that would never forget her father . . . or her mother either. And if she lifted the first little finger against the Pendragons for revenge, it would be more than all my wisdom could do to keep her safe.

Well, it seems a great druid can be more of a fool where women are concerned than I thought.

We came in sight of the poor burnt roofs of Bossiney round. They sounded their war-horns again and the horses broke into a trot and Uther's men burst out with a victory-song. Then Merlyn gave a great whoop, and he kicked his heels into the mare and away we went, galloping in great circles around the dun. There was me clinging on to his waist for dear life, and Uther and Ulfin and Merlyn laughing their heads off and all their army with them. Shameless, they were, coming back to Gorlois's home singing like that, as though his women were cows herded in after a cattle-raid.

Chapter Twenty-Four

When Uther saw the state the place was in, he was all
for taking Ygerne away at once. To be fair to him, he
turned mighty pale when he learned how close his
men had come to roasting her alive. Sometimes, afterwards, I'd pass him looking up at that hall-roof with a
sick, scared look on his face. And if my guts were
twisting worse than usual, I could find myself wishing
he'd got what he deserved.

She wouldn't come with him. Not yet. I knew she
had her reasons.

First, we had to bury Gorlois. Uther pitched a tent
for Ygerne in the Great Meadow, and a snug little
bower it made, with couches of lambskin and striped
hangings at the door. There were shelters for the rest
of us too, and the weather fell warm and blue, so we
took no harm of it, in our bodies. I had a feeling that
we were cattle put out to grass, in place of the herd
we'd lost.

A sore time I had keeping Morgan off her father's
body when they brought him home. A child shouldn't
have seen it, hacked into bloody rags, with the
splinters of bone showing through.

Uther gave Ygerne men, with orders to do whatever she wanted. Then he left us alone with our dead.
Nectan came stalking out of the woods when he'd
gone. A bit pale and hollow-eyed, but he hadn't been

SAMPSON*

harmed. So many good, red-blooded Cornishmen lay dead, but Uther had left those white Christians alive to bury them.

I'll give Ygerne her due, she did Gorlois proud. Well, the way you put your man in the earth says what he was and that tells who you are. There's a deal of boasting even after death. The number of gentry that come, the size of the feast, the height of the stone.

If she'd had her way, she'd have done it in the old style, in a golden chariot, and full armour, with his sword and his shield and his hound, and much more besides. She knew what was fitting. But Nectan stopped all that.

'We brought nothing into the world, we take nothing from it. He has gone to one who offers riches beyond our dreaming.'

What's this world for? Are we supposed to throw it away like a worn-out clout? Nectan spent long enough sitting in his glade beside the pool, playing his harp to the birds. He seemed to like that. What's his heaven if it's more than the best of the best things on earth? Wine and feasting and song . . . and the women beautiful. Couldn't he feel the life that was in the earth he trod on? Life to death and death to life again. That's how it's always been. The dead are here, among the living. We do well to keep them sweet.

But the Christians buried my lord up on the headland beyond Tintagel. Bryvyth came striding up, with all her nuns, singing their litany for the dead. She stood across the grave from Ygerne and scowled at her many a time. My lady had made some sort of peace with Nectan, though I don't know how she did it. But never with Bryvyth. That nun had scolded Gorlois often for his wild ways. But I think she'd loved

178

our black-bearded duke in a queer kind of way, or what passes among those white-blooded women for love. But I couldn't forgive her. She'd denied him what he asked her. She'd cost him his life, and what for? Did she think her prayers were stronger than a man's sharp sword? She hadn't even saved his honour. So I wasn't sorry when she got her come-uppance in the end.

It was a fine day for the funeral, and you could see all the way out to sea as far as Lundy. I heard them shovelling earth on to Gorlois's corpse and I stared across the waves at Tintagel. He might have been there now, wielding his sword on the bridge and laughing through his beard at the whole of Uther's army. Then I looked round for Morgan and I could tell she was seeing him too. Bryvyth was her enemy now along with all the rest.

Afterwards that priest buried Keby and the rest with the same words. As if there was no difference between them.

And then Uther came riding back and married Ygerne. And none too soon. I didn't need to wait for her belly to swell to know why she was looking so pleased with herself.

Uther Pendragon was still for taking her away to one of his palaces up east. But she wouldn't go 'til the child was born. I could have told him why, well enough. She was a beautiful woman, but she wasn't as young and light as she used to be. She wasn't going to appear before all those fine, slender ladies with her waist thickening like a tree-trunk, and too heavy to dance in front of them all. No, she'd wait 'til she had something better than beauty to show off to them. The king's first son. Gorlois had never given her a boy. Three times she'd waited to bear him a child, and each time it had been a girl. And the last time had been bitterest of all. So she'd use every bit of power I'd taught her now.

Well, he built Bossiney up for her again. He had walls made of fine, planked timber, instead of clay and wattle, and hung doors of carved oak, and put on a new thatch as gold as a buttercup. So in the end it was a handsomer place than it had been before. Then he had the walls painted inside with flowers in all the colours you'd see in a summer meadow. He even had the cheek to ask the nuns of Tintagel to embroider hangings for them, for they were known far and wide for pretty needlewomen. He should have known better. Bryvyth was no more afraid of him than she was of Gorlois. She told him no, and I'll bet she gave him the wrong side of her tongue, too. His cheeks turned purple when he got her answer, and the woman who brought it nearly lost an ear. So my lady and her daughters got out their own needles and set to work themselves, meek as you please. I didn't offer to help. There's things I can see far off, and things I can't see under my own nose, and it was fine work. So I stuck to plain stitching and mending.

Still, for all that, he built a chapel on the end of the hall, which was a thing Gorlois had never done. Nectan came and blessed it when it was finished. But there was another that had got in first.

It was the night after they'd dug the trench for the foundation. Something drew me outside to go and look. I caught him at it. He'd put up a circle, but he wasn't troubling to hold it. I stepped right through it, and hardly felt any hurt.

He was just dropping stones in to cover up what he'd done. But not so many that I couldn't see. He smiled at me like a little boy that you've caught with his fingers in the honey-pot.

'Well, Gwennol. We were here first, weren't we? We'll see which of us will have it at the last.'

There was someone else saw what he'd put there. Morgan had followed me. She never asked me what he was doing, or why. She didn't need to.

As soon as the roof of the hall was up, we all moved in and had a great feast. We were pretty merry that night, I can tell you. I looked up at that clean new thatch that hadn't a trace of smoke. And Ygerne's clean new husband, with the blood washed off his hands. But it was Merlyn I mostly had my eye on. He watched them both. I'd seen what he had put under the walls. He meant that hall to stand and he meant that marriage to stand, too. And he understood what had to be given to pay the price. Yet I had a shrewd idea Bossiney wasn't the place he really wanted, nor Uther neither. Time and again I saw them standing out on the headland, looking across at Tintagel Island. Like a baby hanging from its mother by the cord. Well, let them take it from the nuns if they could. I didn't know which would grieve me most. For men to have it that knew the old way, or women who followed the new. Either way, I'd follow what I knew, if I did have to wait till night fell.

Still, it seemed this marriage was going the way Merlyn wanted. I caught him once, running his hands down Ygerne's body just as if she was a figure he had carved himself. She was enjoying it, 'til she looked at his face. Then she pulled away from him saying, 'You may be a great magician, Emrys Merlyn. But there are some things only a woman can do.'

It wasn't his hands on her parts that displeased her. I could see that. It was his looking at her as if she was something he had tooled. Oh, she was very sure of her power just then.

181

So she sat smiling to herself and embroidering, while our sweet Cornish spring turned into a hard, hot summer. Then Uther Pendragon rode away to fight the Saxons.

That frightened her. She would have stopped him if she could. Many a time she'd feared that Gorlois might come back and find her old and barren. But as the years went by she hadn't seemed so worried about him getting killed. Now she'd got her new king, it was a different story. She kissed him bravely enough as she buckled his sword about him. But when he was gone, her pretty face crumpled up and she cried in my arms as she hadn't done since long before Gorlois died.

When I looked up, Merlyn was standing in the shadows, laughing at her without making a sound.

'Little fool,' he said. 'Did you think you could keep him? Do you suppose I gave him into your arms for a plaything? We gamble for higher stakes, the Pendragon and I. The survival of Britain.'

'And so do I!' she rounded on him. 'Do you think I want him dead before his son is born?'

'Born to *what*?' he roared. 'A few stones and bogs? The last black lakes and the sea-lochs of the west? The hollow mountains of the dead? All that will be left of Britain if the red dragon fails!'

She turned white, and put her hands on her belly. She knew the danger she was in now. Her face grew thinner as her body thickened. If Uther should fall, there were few of those fine folk outside Cornwall that knew their new queen or cared about her, and none of Gorlois's kin in Cornwall left to love her.

Merlyn left us too before Midsummer. He was one of those that lean more towards the sun than the moon. He'd have his holy place in those stone circles they call the Giants' Dance.

She turned to me then. She begged me to help her weave a strong spell of safety for Uther's return.

I snapped at her, 'If your spells fail, take yourself to your priest and his prayers! It wasn't me you looked to, to bring a king to you. Why should I help you get him back?'

Well, believe it or not, she went. When she was desperate she'd try anything. I never understood what hold that bloodless saint had over her. What power could he use that wasn't forbidden him? Or was it her that used him? But she'd come back from his cell with some of the lines smoothed out of her face, though there were traces of tears on her cheeks too.

And, may the shade of Gorlois give me peace, I softened a little and put what strength I had left to hers. It wasn't just for the sake of Uther's bright, brown eyes, either. The Pendragon was our king now, and her wedded lord. He was all we had.

He came back, in the heat of summer's end, and mightily pleased with himself. The red dragon was driving the white back. Then the drought broke, and from then on it was teeming rain. We were all shut up in Bossiney, waiting for the child to be born. All except Merlyn. Storm or shine, you could no more hold him in one place than you could trap the wind. He'd be in and out, like the sun on a March day. And where he went to, none of them dared to question.

The days grew short and cold, and the wheel-ruts were full of water, and every dog in the place had mud up to its shoulders. You could leave your shoes by the hearth at night, and in the morning they'd still be cold and sodden.

Our world got very small. We couldn't go out, and the mist was so thick you couldn't see the woods

beyond the gate. It even drove Morgan home from the
cliffs. All summer she'd run wild at the edge of the
sea, with her legs growing longer now, so that it was
more than I could do to keep pace with her. I'd had to
let her go. I'd hoped the sun would heal her wound
and the wind wash her mind clean. But too often I'd
come up with her and find her kneeling on the very
edge of the cliff, staring down at the surf on the rocks
as if she wished herself dead. Now winter had come
and she was like a cat in a cage. The rain made
prisoners of us all. We began to feel as if we were the
only people left in the world.

Seeing King Uther pacing up and down the hall I
used to wonder how long it might be before he got
tired of his new lady. I remembered what they'd told
me about his great cities of stone, like London and
Winchester, and the houses the Romans had built,
with pools of hot water to bathe in. What had we got
to offer but a wooden bucket in a poor wooden dun,
for all it might be a bit grander now than we'd been
used to.

Hours I spent worrying about those fine ladies of
Britain, and how Uther might go rutting after them.
And I thanked my stars the seas were closed as well
as the roads, or I could see he'd have been off. Yet I
never saw the danger under my own nose. A blind old
fool I must have been, too, and never ought to have
been called wise.

My lady – it came hardly to me to say 'the queen' at
first – had sent me to the store-house to fetch more
wool for spinning. I was coming back past the treasury
when I heard the sound of voices inside. A man and a
woman. That pulled me up short. There were none,
only Uther's trusted guard, that had the right to go in
there. Then I shrugged my shoulders and started to

move on. What was it to me now what the queen's women did with the king's soldiers? I'd seen many women this year made widow first and mother after, and maybe by the same man. I wasn't standing out in the cold to bother with them.

It was her laugh that warned me. She hardly bothered to smother it. I'd known that laugh for thirteen years. Well, that moved me sharp enough then. Another step, and I'd have flung that door open and caught them both with their breech-clouts down, and praying I'd be in time to stop the worst.

But as I reached for the latch I heard the man's voice, low but clear enough. The blood left my face. Margawse and Uther Pendragon? I'd known she was shameless, but I never thought it had gone that far. Wouldn't she even stop at the man who was now her father?

I was shaking all over, for to tell you the truth, I was more than a little frightened of the Pendragon, for all his flattering ways. I thought of what Merlyn had warned me, how he was a man that liked to have what he wanted. And I tell you, I felt older and more tired then than I'd ever felt before.

Still I couldn't leave it without knowing the worst. I moved very softly to find a knothole to peep through. He'd got her up against the wall, facing me. I got a glimpse of her white thigh, and her skirt up round her waist. I was squinting round to see how far he'd got himself.

Just then, like a small black cat creeping over the mud, Morgan comes sidling up to me. She must have been watching it all from the shadows of the door across the path. She slipped her hand into mine and looked up at me with a small, sweet smile I hadn't seen much lately.

'You can't stop them, Gwennol. I don't want you to. Don't worry. She doesn't love him, you know. And she doesn't love Mother, either. None of us do. Margawse will avenge Father in her own way.'

And that was a chilly thing for a child of nine to say.

Well, I couldn't stop it. But a few more months and I'd have to give that young woman something to stop what might come from it. I still had power enough for that.

I was back in my lady's bower before Uther was. The fire shone red on Ygerne's face, and when he came in his was red too. He smiled down at her and kissed her long and softly, and put his hand on her belly and down between her thighs. A smile from Uther Pendragon is worth rubies from another man.

Then the door swept open with the wind. But it wasn't Margawse this time. Merlyn was with us again in the firelight. Weeks, he'd been gone from us, and nobody ever asked where he went. But he came dancing in now, dressed all in leather, sewn with little bells that rang when he moved, even to the pointed cap on his head. He looked a proper fool. He rubbed his hands and called for hot wine, and he and Uther Pendragon hugged each other, like a couple of schoolboys wrestling. When they parted, Merlyn looked pretty keenly at Ygerne's belly and smiled to himself when he saw how it had swelled. He always had that cunning look on his face as though it had been his own doing, and not Uther's.

Merlyn stayed close by us then. We were coming to the darkest time of the year. My lady was often tired and resting in bed, but Uther Pendragon always had Margawse and Elaine to laugh and flirt with and keep him company. When the rain fell, they used to get out the chequer-board and play the game of the hunt. I sat in the corner, stitching in the firelight and listening to the harper, 'til my head nodded. What they did when I slept, I shouldn't like to say.

Merlyn sat by the fire with me, watching all of us, or maybe jumping up to show off some trick of his own. I never saw him sleep. I never got used to that. Emrys Merlyn sitting across the hearth from me, as it might have been man and wife. He witched my thoughts, like the rest of them. It wasn't him I should have been thinking of. But what I was worried about was nothing to him. Even he wasn't wise enough to see the harm that was coming of it.

Only Morgan never laughed or played with Uther. She'd rather go to bed early, without light or fire. But often I found her lying awake in the dark.

Chapter Twenty-Five

Midwinter's Eve. In Gorlois's time we used to keep it the proper way. The bonfire should have been stacked on the cliffs and the torch ready to kill the dark and bring the sun to life again, and all of us dancing and drinking around the fire.

But the storm blew and the gale kept us pinned down, like sheep under a hedge. That year I left the kindling of the light to hardier souls than myself. Besides, we had another birth to wait for. Her pains had started. She'd given orders not to let me into her chamber, and that made me angry. But I couldn't help myself. This was my business, before anyone else's. I got my things ready for what had to be done.

We had a bit of cheer in our own hall, but it wasn't like the roof-raising. Our new queen was missing and Uther had a face grey as a snow-cloud. He was striding up and down, up and down all evening, with the drinking-horn in his hand empty as soon as filled. He only stopped to stare at the fine shields and swords he'd hung on our new-painted walls. I dare say he was dreaming of a young hand that might one day hold them. I doubt very much if he was looking at the fine embroideries that Gorlois's daughters had sewed and thinking of their fair hands. He wasn't dreaming of another little maid.

The waiting put him in a sour mood for the dances

and bawdy games that we'd always used to chase away the shadows of winter and put fresh heart into the sun. And to tell you the truth, we were a little shy when it came to dancing the hobby-horse in front of him. The Cornish have always been Horse-people, and he was a Dragon-man, and he still felt like a stranger among us. So it wasn't like it should have been.

Then, like a clap of thunder, he rounded on us and sent us all packing off to bed. Margawse started complaining. She ran to him and threw her arms round his neck, kissing him and trying to wheedle another hour of fun. There are few enough feasts for her liking, and she was the only one, bar the hall-servants, that was truly enjoying herself. But he threw her off as if she was nothing to him now. Elaine had the sense to see there was no arguing with him in this mood, and between us we hushed Margawse and led her off to the sleeping-hut. Morgan had got there before us, but she wasn't undressed, and nothing I could do would make her go to bed before that baby was born . So I worked what I could and waited, 'til I could hardly keep my eyes open, in spite of the draught. And little help I got from Elaine and Margawse.

The child was slow in coming, as though he was her firstborn. But for all it was long, they tell me she had no great pain. And that was a wonder when you think how Morgan nearly killed her, struggling to be born into the light. The Pendragon's child just waited his time.

He came at midnight, as near as I could tell, when the fires were low and the night at its darkest. Hours she had been waiting, Morgan, that was his half-sister, standing there in the wind and the rain, 'til her hair was plastered to her head like seaweed on the rocks.

And then the curtain flew open and the woman's cry went up that it was a boy, and it was all light. Light in

the queen's bedchamber. A great cheer from the hall
and logs thrown on the hearth to make a great blaze,
so that you'd think they were trying to set fire to the
thatch again. And everywhere people running out of
doors into the light to hear the news. Boys as young as
Keby would have been, and women older than me.
Uther went striding off into the queen's bower to
claim his own.

Well, there was more cheering when he came back
to us, looking like the sun itself, and called for more
wine and mead to toast the baby's health. And all the
lot of them went crowding into the hall out of the rain,
even Ruan that had never left my lady's side since the
pains began. She was so proud that night, to see her
you'd think she had dropped the baby herself.

All except one.

When Morgan heard that cry, and knew that the
Pendragon's child was born, and that it was a boy,
she dashed off into the night like a wild thing. I knew
then that I had lost her a second time, and the dark
she'd gone to now was worse than before. I dragged a
cloak over me and stumbled off after her, scolding
and shouting her name. It was wasted breath, what
with the wind tearing my words away and the water
coming over my shoes. She wouldn't have listened,
even if she could have heard me calling. But she was
my little maid, my last baby. I couldn't cut the cord
that bound us together, for all it hurt me.

So there was I, standing out in the storm between
the dark where we'd been and the light where the
new child was, and, believe you me, my cheeks were
wet with more than rain for Gorlois's daughters.
Then Margawse went dashing past towards the hall.
She'd barely the decency to cover her shift. She
wasn't going to be cheated of her wine and merry-

making this time. Well, it took them different ways. Morgan wept, that night and many besides. But I dare say Margawse will laugh when she has her revenge. Elaine keeps her own council.

I felt sorely tempted then to go after Margawse. I like a drop of hot mead as well as anyone, and I was so chilled with wet and cold I was aching in every joint and bone. And traitor you may think me, but I'd worked hard enough with Ygerne to bring that boy into the world. I had something to celebrate now, after all my trouble.

But there was another thirst on me too. Some of you will understand what I mean. It was a long time since I last held a baby in my arms. And none that were given to me to look after had been boys. I was a lively young woman when I took Ygerne from her wet-nurse. I could race on the beach with any lad, and wrestle too. But she'd never had brothers. Or sons, either. And now at last she had done for King Uther what she never did for Gorlois of Cornwall. She had given him a son, a prince of Britain. And the little babe was there, just behind that curtain, lying on the pillow of her bed.

I scratched softly at the door, but I knew no one could hear me for the wind. So I slipped inside. My lady was lying with her eyes closed and her body under the covers as slim as a girl's again. There was only the midwife left, sitting on a stool beside her. And she was nearly asleep after all her work, with a great jug of mead steaming on the floor by her side.

And there on the bed between them, wrapped in white bands, was that precious baby that we had waited for so long. Fair, he was. Handsome. I never saw a child come out of the womb so perfect. Not a wrinkle on him, nor a red mark anywhere. He lay so

peaceful, in a pool of lamplight, with not a thought of
what his coming had cost his sisters. His eyes were
open, looking up at me.

And for all that I might be bitter towards the king
and queen, I lost my heart to their child. He was only a
baby, and it wasn't his fault. When I looked down into
his little face, there wasn't a thought in my head
about Morgan.

Chapter Twenty-Six

Ygerne was looking as pleased with herself as a cat that's found a fat salmon. You could almost hear her purring as she smiled at me. Her hair was brushed out around her on the pillow, like an unbound sheaf of corn. She'd had Ruan bathe and tidy her pretty quickly before the king came, and the lamplight was kind to her. She was beautiful before, it's true, but there was something else glowing through her now. I hadn't seen her as happy as that, not even when she got her pretty Elaine.

Yet I noticed her eyes were a bit anxious, as though she thought it might all be a dream. My hand was reaching out almost by itself, and wanting to stroke that baby's soft cheek, when she caught at my wrist.

'Is he pleased? Gwennol, is the king pleased now?'

I could feel by the tightness of her fingers how much she must have been afraid these nine months. She had taken a high risk. It was like walking over that causeway again. One false step to left or right . . . It might have been a stillbirth, or another girl. But she'd passed the danger, and now her king was waiting on the other side, laughing, with his arms open.

'He's as happy as a boy with his first sword. That is, if he's still sober enough to remember what he's celebrating.'

My eyes strayed to that big jug of mead on the floor.

But it was three parts empty already. The midwife saw my look and pulled it closer to her skirts. She wasn't going to share what she'd earned so dearly, though I could see the glint of gold under her other hand too. Uther would have given her something more lasting to remember him by. He'd be a generous lord to anyone who so much as smiled at him that night, now that he'd got what he wanted. He'd even have slapped the shade of Gorlois on the back if my lord had come back to haunt him.

Ygerne had let go of my wrist. She had the baby in the crook of her arm and she drew him close to her side. The two of them stared up at me. Two pairs of round blue eyes, they were. Smiling. Both half-asleep. I could see there was nothing for me here.

I suppose I could have softened towards her a bit. Stroked her forehead, or kissed her cheek, as if she was still my little maid, and asked her to let me hold the baby. But somehow my pride wouldn't let me. I was dying to touch him. But I wouldn't beg him from her. I don't know how to explain it properly, but I felt as if that boy was ours by rights, and she and Uther had stolen him from us.

So I turned on my heel without telling her about Morgan, and went off over to the hall to soothe my hurt and drink the rest of the night away. It was as hot and noisy as a smith's forge. By the time I'd had two cups of ale inside me, the world looked a rosier place. Elaine was there now, still soft-eyed and pink with sleep. As pretty as her mother. But she'd taken the trouble to put on a proper gown, and braid her hair. Uther had his arm round her. His face was red and his drinking-horn was not as steady as it should be, for all he was a strong man who could hold his liquor well. He'd need helping to bed when morning came. I

196

looked round for a flash of red hair and there was
Margawse, with her shift unlaced at the neck under
her scarlet cloak, flirting with half a dozen of Uther's
young warriors.

There was someone else too. Crouched on the stones
in the corner of the hearth, as if the cold had got right
into his bones. Merlyn. It's a funny thing, but he
seemed a different person each time you saw him. He
was a man that came and went. You never knew
when or how you would see him next.

He was here now, all right. But not looking at all like
what I'd expected him to do on such a night. He had
an old goatskin pulled round his shoulders, that stank
to high heaven, and the rest of his clothes were in
rags. A proper beggar, he looked. But what gave me a
start was how old he seemed. Older than I'd thought
he could have looked, for a man that usually carried
himself so tall and moved as if he was going to break
out into dancing at any moment. He wasn't dancing
now. And it wasn't lime that made his hair look white
this time. It was as if that little boy that had just come
into the world had drained all the life out of him and
left him an old man.

He saw me coming and raised his beaker to me. I
wondered then if he had Margawse's fever, for his
eyes were red and watery. He hardly had the strength
to lift his arm.

That cheered me up and put a bit of pride back into
me. I felt a bit like Ygerne then, and there must have
been a pretty broad grin on my face when I walked up
to him.

'Well,' I said. 'You may have brought the stallion to
our mare. But there are some things even Emrys
Merlyn can't do. It needed woman's wisdom to bring
this foal into the world.'

Me, pulling Merlyn's leg, like a milkmaid with a farmhand. I must have been drunk already. He sounded so weary as if it cost him an effort to talk.

'There are many things that Emrys Merlyn cannot do, or the world would not be as it is. And where were you, Gwennol Far-Sight, when this foal was dropped?'

That made me wince. He meant it to.

'I was working my weft, never your fear. I still have power, though I get little thanks for it these days.'

'I told you, Gwennol. We should be allies. Our time is passing. A little space of sunshine before the storm comes. I need your help.'

'Me? Help the Pendragon?'

'Not him. All *this*.'

He stared out then with a wild, flashing sort of look in his eyes, as if the walls weren't there and it wasn't pitch-black night. There was no telling how far he could see across the land.

I couldn't understand what he meant. I was looking round for something else. And what I was hoping to see was a draggled black thing, like a half-starved cat, that might have crept in out of the storm at last for a bit of shelter and comfort. But I hadn't much faith I'd find her here, and I was right. No matter where I looked, there wasn't a sign of Morgan. Still, I worked my way round the crowd thinking she might have slipped into one of the side stalls where Uther's warriors slept, and curled up in the straw. I found more than a few merry couples enjoying themselves but I couldn't find her. Fuddled I might be, but I started to worry where she might have got to on such a night as this. I could curse my way past a closed gate after dark even now, if I had to, though Uther's warriors were not so feared of me as Gorlois's Cornish boys had been. A little maid like Morgan couldn't. But she didn't need to. She was as nimble as a cat. I knew she could be over that rampart in two shakes of a duck's tail. And who was going to stop her in the dark? She could be on the cliffs by now. I pushed that thought away. It was like watching a rat poke its head out of the wall, and then turning your back and trying to pretend to yourself that you haven't seen it.

I needed another beaker of ale. As I pushed my way back round the hall I saw two figures, like giants they were, on the dais. The fire was throwing their shadows high on the wall behind them. Uther was leaning his fist on the high table to hold himself upright, and Merlyn was standing over him now. He was drawn up to his full height again. It struck me then that Merlyn was the taller of the two, though Uther Pendragon was a big man. Merlyn didn't look old now, though his hair was white, and he was the only sober man in the room. He had a clear, singing voice. He kept it low, but I could hear it through all the shouting.

'You made a promise, Uther. On the honour of your father's grave you vowed the boy to me before ever he was conceived. It was a fair bargain. I have fulfilled my part. Now keep yours.'

Uther's fist thumped down on the table. But he wasn't sober enough to keep it steady.

'But he's my son! My only child.' The drink was slurring his speech. He'd be crying soon.

'And therefore most precious and most vulnerable. Our time is shorter than you think. These days are dangerous. I must have the boy. Soon.'

'When?'

But Merlyn looked up and saw me watching. And ill though he'd looked, in three strides he was across the

199

hall like a hawk swooping. He towered over me, and I
was mortally afraid. His eyes glittered, and not with
firelight either. He gripped my arm like a noose round
a hare's neck.

'Gwennol Far-Sight! So it seems your ears pierce
the distance as well as your eyes.'

We weren't allies now. We were no milkmaid and
farmhand.

'I was only watching out for my young ladies, sir.'

His eyes swung round the hall, and he muttered
under his breath, 'Elaine. Margawse.' Then his
fingers tightened on my arm, 'til I fairly yelped. 'And
where is Morgan?'

I couldn't meet his eyes.

'It all happened so quick. When the baby was born
she went dashing off into the storm like a mad thing.
That great fool of a man . . .'

'The baby! The queen's bower? Are you sure she's
not there?'

A blacksmith's pincers couldn't have gripped me
harder.

'No, sir. It was the first place I looked. There was
only the midwife with them. And the little babe was
dropping asleep, bless him.'

I didn't tell him it wasn't any thought of Morgan
that had taken me there. His hand let go of my arm
and he seemed to draw his breath a bit easier. But he
wasn't satisfied yet.

'I have business to finish with Uther. Find her,
Gwennol. And watch her well these next few days. I
warn you, do not forget Morgan. Even for a moment.'

He didn't exactly push me out of the hall. But he
looked at me so stern that, I don't know why, I turned
and went out into that storm without another word.
Merlyn wasn't a man you said no to.

200

All the same, when I came to, I wasn't best pleased at finding myself the wrong side of that door again. I'd never had that last beaker of ale and it was sheeting down with rain. I looked in our sleeping-hut, but she wasn't there. So I crossed the path to the queen's chamber again, just to make sure.

My heart was beating fast as I opened the door.

They were all three asleep. Ygerne with her face half-buried under her hair. The midwife rolled on the floor, snoring. And that sweet baby tucked up in a wicker cradle all threaded prettily with ribbons of gold.

There was no one to see me now, so I bent my old stiff back and reached out my hands to take him up.

I never heard her coming, but her shadow fell over the basket and made the baby blink. I felt who it was, like a chill in the room when the wind has changed. She was standing close behind me. The water was running out of her hair in rivers, and her dress was black with rain. But she smiled at me sweetly. Oh, very sweetly she smiled!

'Poor Gwennol.' she said. 'Did you think he would be your baby? Did you think they would give him to you when the wet-nurse has finished with him? Were you dreaming of dressing him, and playing with him, and singing him to sleep, as you did with Gorlois's daughters? Don't you know who he is? He's the eldest son of the King of all the Britons. He'll be the greatest prince in the land soon. Fine ladies will feed him gruel. Court bards will sing him lullabies. And the wisest scribes in Christendom will teach him. Did you think they would leave him here in Bossiney with you?'

Oh, she was clever for nine years. Like a hot poker to the eyes it was. Yes, I'd been a foolish old body, dreaming what I had dreamed. And it didn't hurt any the less for knowing she was right. It was the way the child did it. She knew she was all I had left now, but she'd enjoyed bringing tears to my eyes. They'd killed the light of her life, so she'd put out the light for the rest of us.

Her voice woke Ygerne up. She opened her eyes and saw her daughter.

'What is it?' she said, and you could see her move quick to gather the baby close to her. But the pillow was empty. Well, her eyes went wide with fear.

But Morgan laughed and swooped for the cradle. She had the baby in her arms before any of us could stop her. Then she looked up at us with her green eyes, as wide and innocent as you please.

'What's the matter with you all? What are you staring at? He's my little brother, isn't he?'

She bent her black hair over his face and we thought she was kissing him. Then the baby let out a yell. And when that maid lifted her head, there on his tiny white neck were the red marks of her teeth.

Chapter Twenty-Seven

Those few short days before Christmas I never had an easy moment. I'd been used to letting Morgan run free. She was a child that needed to be left on her own. In summer, as long as she didn't wander into the forest, I'd let her play where she wanted amongst the bramble brakes or paddle her way through the pools on the beach. Just so long as she didn't get quite out of my sight. She might seem to be reckless, but she never came to harm that way. It was Margawse I'd worried about. Tossing her red hair and flashing her green eyes at every man in the dun.

But now I had worse than that to fear. I had lost my little Morgan that I had wept over so many nights when we never thought she would live to see nine summers. When I looked at her white face now since the year had turned, it was just as if there was a stranger in the room. And no child either. Hours she would sit silent, brushing her black hair 'til it shone like a chough's wing and cleaning her nails. And where was my little maid that used to run home to me with her hair tangled in the wind and her hands full of sea-shells?

And then suddenly I'd look up and she would be gone, like a soul out of the body. Only her empty stool beside the door. My blood turned cold each time and the first place I'd run would be my lady's rooms. Her women would be there, or the wet-nurse, and that sweet boy that still had no name, and all looking as peaceful as a field of lambs in spring. And there I'd stand panting in the doorway like a silly old fool, staring at them. And as like as not, when I got back to our own hut Morgan would be there, sewing in the light from the doorway. She'd lift her green eyes and smile at me. But there wasn't any warmth in her smile now, and no kindness either.

Still, she hadn't learned to be deceitful then, though there were others who'd deceived her cruelly. Sometimes she would sit scowling over her work, then jump up suddenly and laugh in my face. She'd be off like a greyhound, straight to her mother's room for everyone to see. And all the women would start to their feet and pull their skirts away from her. They all feared her. The one that was nearest would snatch up the baby, and Morgan would burst into laughter at their looks. She enjoyed frightening us. But I wonder now if she hadn't been crying out to us to stop her.

Hours, I lay awake worrying over her. For who was there to keep her now from harm? Merlyn had the strength, I didn't doubt that, but he'd sooner have cursed her than taught her what he knew. I even thought about the white nuns on Tintagel. Yes, you may stare at me. But they hadn't saved her father, or her mother either. There was only me.

I was sorely tempted then. I knew where there was healing for her hurt. I had led her mother and sisters down that way. But when it came to Morgan, still I drew my hand back. There was this strong feeling on me, as if there was a barrier across the path that I daren't cross. I knew that once I took the first step down that road with her, that way would lead deeper than I wanted to go. Deeper than I'd been myself. And who knows what would come of it? It frightened me. So I held my peace. I don't know if I did right.

Still, I couldn't be watching her all the time. Morgan had hurt me deep, saying what she had about the baby. But it was no more than the truth. He wouldn't be with us long. Who's to blame me if my feet were sometimes straying to that bower when Ygerne's back was turned?

On Christmas Eve, Merlyn, that had been with us since the boy was born, packed his bags to go. It was a strange time to be taking to the road, but that was the way he was. He never said where he was going and we didn't ask. We crowded round him in the yard as they saddled his white mare, and the two of them were dancing about as if they were in a hurry to be gone. The wind had changed. It was blowing from the north now, chasing the rain away and freezing the puddles.

And just as we thought he was ready to ride off, there was a flurry of white in the gateway, like a shower of hail.

Nectan, with his cloak blowing round him. Come to shrive us all before the feast of Christmas. Well, what those Christians call a feast. To tell you the truth, I'd forgotten about their holy day. I had so much else on my mind, good and bad, just then.

We were coming into their time now. It was too raw weather for his bell to gather everyone in the open air. There'd be candles in the chapel and the hall. He'd spread his table with a fair cloth, a book, a chalice and a dish. And he'd make our rafters ring with his hymns. A very different sort of singing from Midwinter's Eve, that would be, though he did it gladly enough. It always surprises me, that folk that live so thinly can sing so heartily as that. Uther's warriors would make a brave sound singing with him.

205

Then I turned my head, and I saw something that startled me. Merlyn had forgotten the Christians too, or I could tell he'd have gone sooner. It had struck me often that when the chapel bell called us for Sunday or a Christian feast-day, Merlyn always contrived to be somewhere else.

There was a cloud passed over his face when he saw that lean saint coming, and it made me feel queer for a moment. He looked so old. I don't just mean tired and white, like he had after the boy was born. No, worse than that. You'll think me daft but you might have seen such a look if you'd invited the Old Ones to join you at Samain, and the Older Ones had come in their place. The ones our own gods drove under the hollow hills when they took the land.

I thought Nectan checked too at the sight of Merlyn. He crossed himself. I don't think he was afraid. More like a man buckling on his armour. Though I wouldn't have blamed him if he had to screw up his courage. Then he gathered his muscles together and came on. They didn't say anything. Just looked at each other, eye to eye, like two warriors before a battle.

Yes, I thought. That fool of a hermit should have listened when Gorlois warned him.

It didn't last long. I don't think anybody saw it but me. Next moment a smile broke out on Nectan's face, and he turned to Uther.

'Well, your honour? Is your new son keeping healthy this cold weather? I must talk with you about his christening.'

Uther clapped him on the back and laughed.

'All's well with the queen and her son, thank the Lord. Go in and warm yourself by the fire. They're ready for you in the chapel. Give us a moment to bid farewell to Emrys Merlyn.'

The saint thanked him and strode indoors out of the frost.

I had known Merlyn for a man that was very sure of himself. He was like a piper that could make all of us dance to his tune. And he was always quick with a jest or a clever word. But I saw for a moment he didn't know what to do when the saint spoke of the christening. He almost looked as if he was thinking of unpacking his saddle-bags. Then he grinned at us sudden, with that queer one-sided smile of his.

'I don't wait to give my gifts 'til Christmas Day,' he said.

And I knew then I was right. I don't doubt he had his plans to make for the boy, but we shouldn't see him again until the psalms and the prayers were over.

But he wouldn't let the Pendragons forget him. He reached down into his saddle-bags and drew out something for all of them. Fine, feast-time gifts they were. He gave Margawse a bronze mirror. Beautifully patterned on the back, it was, with leaves and song-birds' heads. I knew she'd be hours admiring her pretty face in it. And for Elaine he had a little case with fine bone needles, and a pair of scissors shaped like a swan's beak, and skeins of coloured silks, that made her turn pink with pleasure. Uther got a set of dice in a silver cup, and Ygerne a golden comb. I didn't see what he handed her for the baby.

I must have been as daft as the rest of them, pressing round him, hoping for a smile before he said goodbye. His eyes met mine. Grey eyes, he had, like the blade of a fine sword. He looked at me keenly. And when he did smile, I felt the thrust of it deep inside my belly.

'Come here, Gwennol,' he said, and reached into his leather satchel again. 'This is for you.'

Well, I gasped. I'd never expected him to give me
anything. A red shawl, it was, that he told me was
made of goat's hair. I stood with it over my arm,
stroking it, for I'd never had anything of my own so
fine and soft, and I could feel the warmth of it already
in the cold wind. I know he laughed at my face. Years,
I kept that shawl.

When it came to Morgan's turn I was sure she
wouldn't be there to see him off. But she was standing
a little way off, leaning against the doorpost of our
hut, watching us from the shadows that were blue
with frost. Merlyn took out a little hunting-knife, with
the bone handle carved like a boar, all bristles and
tusks. It was a rare piece of craft. He held it out to
her.

'For Morgan to stab us all in the heart with,' he
said. And the smile never got past his mouth.

Last Christmas Morgan would have loved a present
like that more than any pretty thing her sisters had.
Wasn't Gorlois the finest huntsman in all Cornwall?
And didn't she ride at his heels whenever he would
take her? She'd have run straight off with that knife
and played that she was the son her father always
wanted.

But Gorlois was dead. And this Morgan was a
stranger to us. She'd never hunted with Uther.

She said angrily, 'That's a boy's present. I'm a
woman now.'

Though she wasn't yet. Not as I understand it, anyhow. Merlyn knew that too. He smiled down at her
slowly, and even, I thought, a bit sadly.

'When Morgan, daughter of Gorlois, becomes a
woman, then the whole of Britain will have something
to fear.'

She looked at him and there was doubt in her face,

208

as if she feared he was laughing at her. She let the
knife fall to the ground between them. Then she turned
her back and went inside our hut.

'Watch her,' he said to me sharply.

He took my arm then, over that red shawl, and his
eyes held mine.

'A little time we must keep him safe, Gwennol. A
few more days. And then you may leave the future to
me. Watch Morgan.'

I knew what he meant, though I was too choked to
answer him.

Then he kicked his heels into the mare's sides and
cantered out of the gate with everyone waving and
calling after him.

When he was past the oak I turned my eyes away. I
was quicker to be rid of him then than I had been that
first time. I remembered I had to pick up the knife. It
was too fine a thing to be left lying in the mud. But
someone else had got there first.

Nectan had come out into the yard again. He was
holding the knife out to Morgan. It seems they were
the only two in the whole dun who hadn't been caught
up in Merlyn's glamour.

'This is yours, I think,' he said. He smiled at her
pretty kindly for a childless man. 'It's a good blade.
You could whittle a piece of boxwood with it to make
an angel for the Christ-child's crib.'

She turned away from him without a word, as she
had from Merlyn.

He must have felt me watching. He faced slowly
round.

'Well,' I said, with a grim sort of smile. 'The son of a
holy virgin, is it?'

He had the grace to laugh, though there wasn't
much humour in it.

'Yes, Gwennol Far-Sight. You have the better of me there. I was a fool. Too trusting. But we grow wiser. He has run away and I am here. Uther will trust his child to me. And whose side are you on, Gwennol? Will you help me care for the child?'

I smiled at him, as innocent as you please.

'I have always cared for the child, sir. Since the day she was born.'

Fool of a man. He never even noticed.

He held out the knife to me.

'Will you give it to Morgan?'

He had bigger things to think about than that. So he never saw, as I did, that she had turned her head and was staring after him with a sort of hunger in her face.

I'll never forgive him for that. She'd seen he wasn't afraid of Merlyn. She might have turned to him then.

Yes! Don't hiss at me. I'd rather he had taken her for his Church, if it had made her happy.

But it was only the boy that mattered to any of them.

Merlyn had gone. Those that cared to told Nectan their sins. Then we sang their hymns, and made ready for another child's coming.

When it was done I went back to the sleeping-hut. Morgan was there. She was holding Margawse's mirror and smiling at her own reflection as she touched her hair. That gave me a start. Just for a moment she looked like a small, dark copy of her mother. Then she heard me coming and put the mirror down. She picked up Elaine's sewing-case and began to play with the scissors. I heard her draw her breath sharp. When I looked down, one of those dainty blades had pierced her finger, drawing blood.

But the hunting-knife lay on the chest beside her bed where I had left it. She never touched it.

Chapter Twenty-Eight

We kept that Christmas as we never had before. And it was the first of many days' feasting. Uther was as pleased with himself as a dog with two tails, and both of them wagging fit to bust. He carried the baby round the hall for everyone to say how handsome he was and how like his father. Tiny though that mite was, he dandled him on his knee through the mummers' play and the horse's dance and all the sword-swinging in the hall. He couldn't be done with showing him off to the world. I never saw a man tempt the gods so, not even Gorlois, and he was proud enough. In the end I couldn't stand it. I snatched the child off him and took him back to his mother. Let Uther show off his daughters now.

Well, as soon as he'd finished toasting his son he gave it out that he meant to marry Margawse off like Elaine to a king up north, beyond the Wall. They'd be betrothed just as soon as spring came and ships could sail north again to seal the bargain. I think he knew as well as I did we'd need to be quick about it. Margawse had come to her womanhood these last few days.

I didn't grieve over her when I heard the news. There never was a girl I'd be gladder to see wed. I'd had enough of her light-headed ways. Though it was no liege-man of Uther's she'd be marrying, by the sound of it, but a king that he had need to be better friends with. He'd sell Gorlois's filly off at a fair price, to keep the north at peace. At least I needn't fear her shaming us much longer.

And still the Pendragon's boy had no name. There were some that held that he was safer so. What has no name can't be named, and no one can get power over it. But some of the Christians had a different view of it. They said it was a dangerous time. If a child should die unchristened, their Heaven would have none of it, and it would become a pixie spirit, wandering the moors and leading baptised folk astray. But Nectan wouldn't have it was so. And I could have told them there were worse things than babies loose on the moor at night.

But we had no fears that this child would die before its time. You never saw a healthier baby. Day after day we watched him grow. His little cheeks were pink and full and his eyes bright and clear, and the winter sunlight seemed to catch in his hair. He was a child of the light, that one. Every day he grew stronger, like the sun. Many a time I'd make some excuse for passing the door so I could put my head round the curtain and have a look at him lying in his cradle. And if no one was looking, I'd pick him up and cuddle him, and croon in his ear the songs I used to sing his mother. We had no snow that winter, though it froze hard. But for once I was casting charms to make it long and bitter, with snowdrifts up to the roof. When the spring came, I knew what would happen. They would mount their horses and chariots, and Ygerne would take her son up in her arms, as proud as you please, and they would be gone, out of Cornwall.

Still, no good crying about it 'til it happened. We would make a great feast for him while he was still ours. So we kept that midwinter season as never

212

before. I must say that Uther Pendragon was a
merrier man than ever Gorlois had been, and a richer
one too. It was a gay time we had, and Elaine and
Margawse looked as merry as their mother, whatever they felt inside.

The boy was to be named on what they call the feast
of Epiphany. Nectan had planned it. A double cele-
bration, that would be, for the baptism of the King of
Heaven and for King Uther's firstborn son. Uther had
sent word to all the lords and ladies in Dumnonia to
come to the christening, if the roads would let them.
Bossiney had never seen anything like it in all my
days. The kitchens were busy baking and brewing
and roasting 'til the steam came out of the thatch so
thick and wholesome you could almost taste it. Both
hall and chapel were decked with armfuls of holly
and ivy. And so many lamps everywhere, you'd think
they'd never have found oil and fat enough for them
all.

Uther thought he had Nectan dancing to his tune,
though I wasn't so sure myself. The saint might seem
pretty thick with the king and queen these days, but it
was his own battle he was fighting with Merlyn over
the boy. They were all the same. They only thought
about him. But there was one thing made Uther
frown. There was someone he could never wrap
round his little finger, for all his bright eyes and
golden gifts. Bryvyth had been bidden to the christening, with all the other high lords and ladies round
about. She might live plainly, but she was a mighty
learned woman, and they treated her just the same
as if she'd been a bishop. And now she had sent back
word from Tintagel she wouldn't come. Things had
been done there that couldn't be mended. And that
boy was at the heart of it. Uther and Ygerne made

213

more show of treading the Christian way than ever
Gorlois had done. They might fool Nectan, but it did
them no good with Bryvyth. The Church was never
best friends with the Pendragons.

So we came to Twelfth Night, and the boy was to be
named in the morning. And as if I wasn't busy enough
already, Margawse went down with the fever. It was
nothing more than a winter chill, and she was as
strong as a horse. But there was no one but me to
nurse her, and she was as cross as a dog that's lost its
bone because she was missing the last days of the
feast. She couldn't bear to be dull. And how I was
supposed to see to her and keep my eyes on Morgan is
more than I can tell. I took Elaine aside and told her to
watch her little sister closely and see she never left
the hall. But you'd need to be as watchful as an owl
and as fast as a hawk to keep up with that one. Elaine
was no match for her. She put me in mind of a plump
house-cat that keeps to the warmth of the fire and
doesn't like to get her fur dirty in the mud.

I wished Merlyn had stayed. Bryvyth spoke true
enough when she said he was a strange soul-friend
for a Christian king. He was as slippery as a trout. I
knew the times and the reasons, and I could guess
better than most some of the places he went. And
Merlyn knew that I knew. Many's the time he got up
from the bench and looked at me before he went out of
the hall with that quick half-smile in his eyes. And I
always felt that if I'd been only a little bit younger he
might have pulled me by the hand and whipped me off
with him. It's a strange thing to say, but I was never
sure whether he and I were friend or foe.

But surely he'd be back for the christening? He'd
had a way of talking to Uther almost as if the baby
belonged to him.

It fell dark early on the eve of Epiphany. The wind was rising 'til you could almost feel the earth shaking beneath you where the great waves were flinging themselves against the land. There was no rain with it this time. It would be bright moonlight a bit later on, if only the wind could tear a hole in the clouds. They were pressed thick across the sky now, like a black herd of galloping cattle.

The feasting-hall looked a brave sight across the yard, with all the lamps burning and the fire leaping up the logs. But there'd be no games for me that night. I was left sitting by Margawse's bedside. They sent us food, goose-meat and mead, and a bowl of good broth for Margawse. But it wasn't the same. There's no fun in getting drunk by yourself. I missed the company. It's a hard life we lead at Bossiney, though it was a sight gayer since King Uther was our lord, and midwinter had always been a time for laughter and a bit of horseplay and plenty to eat and drink. And what's the harm in that, even at my age, if it helps to see us through the dark of winter?

And besides, I couldn't have eyes everywhere. I'd sent Morgan off to the hall with her sister Elaine, both of them with their skin washed and the grease sponged off their best gowns and their hair plaited with silk braids. As quiet and demure as a little queen Morgan looked that night. But by now there wasn't one of us that knew what was going on behind those green eyes. So I wasn't easy.

Supper never seems to take so long when you eat it by yourself. I licked the grease off my fingers and picked my teeth and listened for the harp and the singing and the dancers' pipes. The music seemed to come and go between gusts of wind, like the sea. The mead was making me drowsy, but I could tell well enough when the food was finished and the horseplay began, by the noise. A great roar of singing and stamping. And no court bard's ditty, either, I can tell you. And they shouted louder than ever when it was finished. They'd be lucky if there weren't daggers out before the night was over, with all the wine and mead and beer I'd seen them taking into the hall. And in the morning, they'd all of them be nursing sore heads and walking to chapel like sober gentlefolk to see the baby prince baptised with his new Christian name. And he? He'd be fast asleep now, bless him, and not caring a bit for the noise they were making over his coming.

It didn't surprise me when Elaine came back early. She was never one for rough play and bawdy jokes, and there'd be plenty of that tonight. It would have been enough of a treat for her to serve the wine to Uther's guests at the high table in her mother's place. She was fourteen now. Her breasts were filling out and her cheeks thinning. She'd make a proper queen before long. But I was angry when I saw she hadn't brought Morgan.

'Where's your sister?' I said sharply. 'You haven't left her, have you, when I told you never to take your eyes off her?'

She tossed her head a bit more proudly than she used to. She had more than a little of her mother in her.

'You forget, I had more important things to look to, with so many guests.' Then she laughed and hugged me, like the old times. 'Don't worry, Gwennol. She wanted to stay and watch the sword-dancing. It's all right. Mother's still there with her.'

'And much good that will do,' I muttered.

It wasn't Morgan our queen would have her eyes on. In Gorlois's time she was more delicate. She'd have gone to bed earlier, with the baby so newly-born. But she was bolder now that she was Uther's wife. And who was I to blame her? I'm old enough to be her mother, and I'd sooner have been in the hall with the rest of them than stuck in the bed-chamber. Ygerne had come late to her crown, and she meant to have her fill of it.

Elaine must have known what I was thinking, for she said, 'Go on, Gwennol. Why don't you go and enjoy yourself? Margawse is asleep, and I'll be here if she wakes. And you can watch Morgan for yourself.'

I didn't need telling twice. I've never missed Twelfth Night. I'll sit down to a feast, any time. Old Religion or Christian, it's all the same to me, so long as there's plenty of food and drink and dancing.

As soon as I got to the hall I looked for Morgan. And she had gone from the table. I could feel the panic starting inside me. There was her mother laughing, and the king beside her. I looked everywhere. And then I saw her. Like a little black shadow in the corner by the hearth, behind the harper. Well, let her stay there. If the play got rough, she'd be out of the way of it there.

Oh, it was good to be squashed up on the bench among friends, and the warmth of their bodies better than any fire. There was still drink going round, and some scraps of food left, and I went on stuffing 'til I lost a tooth cracking nuts. They plunged hot iron in the mead, and passed it round fizzing hot. We were all more than a little merry.

Then the dogs began barking outside. All the men leaped up and reached for their swords, because who would be on the road in the dark, when the gates were shut and the yard-dogs loosed and food on the table? But we recognised that voice calling to the dogs

217

through the wind. King Uther laughed.

'All's well,' he said. 'It's only Merlyn, come late to join our feast.'

Merlyn. On the eve of the holy-day of Epiphany? So he'd come back to battle with Nectan for the boy, had he?

The door crashed open, and the wind almost took the platters off the table. Merlyn stood there. He was dressed like a druid, in a white gown with bands of gold across his breast. He had a wreath of holly woven round his cap. But there was no smile on his face now. We just sat there gaping at him like fools. You could see his eyes going round the hall, and I shivered as they went over me. But they came to rest on Ygerne.

'Where is your child?' he roared at her.

And never mind that she had four.

Her hand flew to her mouth. She was as drunk and foolish as the rest of us. She didn't understand what he meant. But I did. Maybe I hadn't had time to drink as much as the rest, or maybe I'd seen more than was good for me. But my eyes went straight to the corner by the fire, and it was empty. Merlyn saw my face.

'And where is Morgan!' Like a river bursting into a house, his voice was.

He was running out of that door before I could get to my feet. He was in the queen's chamber by the time I came panting in. When I pushed past him I was mortally afraid of what I was going to see.

At first I thought the room was empty. Then I saw the wet-nurse, lying in her cot, dead-drunk. And that was all. The cradle was bare. No Morgan. No sign of blood.

Chapter Twenty-Nine

Ygerne let out such a scream, you could have heard it all the way to Land's End. But I'd feared worse than what I saw.

'Thanks be! At least she hasn't killed him.'

I don't think that boy's mother even knew what I meant. Wise woman or no, she'd been so besotted with her fine king she hadn't the wit to see what she was doing to her own daughters.

She was standing there, with her hand to her mouth and her blue eyes staring, crying, 'My baby! Where has my baby gone!'

Merlyn turned on her. I'd never seen him so angry, and it made me quail, I can tell you.

'This is at your door! Vain, foolish woman! I thought we were agreed. I gave you two kings. Was that too much for one woman to hold?'

'Guard your tongue!' King Uther shouted at him 'It is your queen you speak to.' But there were few of us that had much time for Ygerne that night. 'You, Gwennol! Is this Morgan's work?'

'Who else?' said Merlyn.

'By God! I should have sent the bitch to join her father!'

'Gwennol Far-Sight,' said Merlyn, gripping my wrists and looking into my eyes. 'Where would she take him?'

'Down to the sea,' I said, like a woman in a dream. I never stopped to think how I knew it.

Uther Pendragon was out of the door like a shot. Merlyn snatched up a fur from the bed and threw it round me. Then he gripped me by the elbow and bundled me out into the storm. My lady was left behind in a flood of tears. But there were plenty of folk crowding round to fuss over her.

'Which way?' shouted Merlyn. He had his mouth close to my ear, but I could hardly hear him for the gale.

I couldn't tell him. I had this picture in my mind, like the one thing you remember from a dream after you wake up. But where it was, I'd no notion. One wet rock looks much the same as any other on a stormy night.

So I set off as if I was going down to Bossiney Haven, because that's the nearest way to the beach. I could hardly walk for the wind. I had Uther Pendragon on one side of me and Merlyn on the other, and they were fairly carrying me along. When I looked back there were soldiers with drawn swords behind us. And all for a little girl not ten years old. Some of them had lanterns, though they hardly needed them. There was a queer sort of cloudy moonlight, between dark and light.

We hadn't gone far before I stopped. I couldn't say why, but I knew something was wrong. She hadn't come this way. I felt a power drawing me, and I knew she must have felt it too. I could tell now where she'd gone, all right.

There was a good deal of swearing and grumbling when we turned round. We went stumbling back over stones and potholes. But I made them follow me. I was like a hound that's picked up a fresh scent. Then the moon broke loose and we were up on the downs on the edge of the cliff, making for Tintagel.

Merlyn struck his thigh a great blow. And I could tell he was cursing himself this time for a slow-witted fool.

I'd have been plucked right over the cliff if I hadn't had those two tall men on either side of me, holding on. There was a sort of silver mist all round us, though the moon and stars were bright over our heads. The waves were crashing so hard against the cliffs they were sending the spray right up into our faces.

We were almost running now. Sometimes the wind seemed to push us back like a great flat hand. Other times it would come swirling round so I thought it would pick us up and carry us flying. All the time we were drawing nearer to that holy island.

But she wouldn't be there. It wasn't those white nuns she was running to tonight. She wouldn't cross that causeway a second time. I knew what drew her, though I'd never told her a word about it. She didn't need my teaching.

There was a way down to the beach before you reach that terrible bridge. It was a gully, running with water, and rough walking. The lower we got the wetter it was, with the spray coming down on us like rain. The roar of the waves was so loud it mazed your thoughts. I turned colder inside than out. For how could my Morgan and that precious mite be safe on the rocks in such a storm?

Then we got to the bottom and the cliffs sheltered us a bit from the wind. But we could still hardly hear ourselves speak, for the brook was hurling itself off the ledge in a great waterfall.

We could see the waves breaking on the point, shooting high walls of water up into the air, and the flung spray turning to silver in the moonlight. But the bay was quieter. A great black swell was running in. Like hump-backed serpents coming at us, it looked. It dashed itself against the rocks with a hiss a bit softer than the crashes out on the point. The tide was full in. There wasn't a foot of beach you could put a dry foot on. I knew where Morgan had tried to take him, all right. But the Mother's Hole would be full to the roof with the sea now, and the stone in the middle drowned deep by two currents of water. She couldn't have got further than this.

I'd lost her heart long ago. But when I looked at those black shining walls of water rearing up towards us, I thought I'd lost her poor little body too.

Then we saw her. She was standing on a high pinnacle of rock with the waves pounding all around her. How she got there, dear only knows. We wouldn't have seen her, for the water was as black as the mouth of hell, and Tintagel behind her was dark, as if it had turned its back on us. If there was a glimmer of light anywhere on it, we couldn't have seen it through the spray. Likely those nuns were safe in bed, like the good Christians most of them were. Still, for the first time in my life I found myself wishing that Bryvyth Crook-Staff might be awake and praying for us, up there in the dark. We needed all the power we had between us that night.

Even then we couldn't have seen Morgan with her black hair and her gown dark with wetting. But she had a little white bundle clutched to her chest, and just then the wind blew back her sleeves and showed her two white arms.

I must have drawn my breath sharpish. I heard Merlyn hiss between his teeth, so I knew he'd seen her too. But neither of us dared to utter a word.

222

Merlyn waved his hand at the men behind us to be
still, though to tell you the truth, you couldn't have
heard an army marching over the stones above those
breakers. It was Uther broke the spell. He was
always a man that couldn't bear to wait, never mind
what it cost afterwards.

He swore a great oath and let go of my arm. And he
drew his sword so fast it's a wonder it didn't take the
head off my shoulders.

'Morgan!' he roared. 'Give him back to me this
instant, or I'll skewer you like a sucking pig.'

My heart was in my mouth when he yelled at her
like that. I knew her better than he did. A curse like
that might have been all she was waiting for. I truly
thought we'd seen the last of those two children then.

But she didn't even seem to have heard him at first.
Still and black she was, like a woman carved out of
bog-wood. And the ends of the baby's white bands
fluttering in the wind like prayer-rags.

'Morgan!' he thundered at her.

The wind dropped just then, so that his voice came
echoing back off the cliffs.

She turned her head, and looked over her shoulder
towards us.

'If you come one step closer, I'll drop him into the
sea.'

My heart fairly broke for her when she said that. I
knew what it meant. If she'd really wanted to kill her
brother, it would have only taken her a moment. She
needn't have carried him all the way through the
storm to here. One stab with that hunting-knife
Merlyn had given her, and it would have been all over
and done with. His little life-blood running away on
the bedchamber floor, and the Pendragons punished.

But she hadn't killed him yet. I think she couldn't do

223

it unless they drove her now. How long had she been standing up there on that rock in this wild storm, holding her baby brother in her arms? I knew where she had been trying to take him, all right. But why had she held on to him for so long? Then it came to me that she was like a frightened black kitten trapped on a roof, and mewing for someone to come and help her down. I think there were two souls in her. One of them was wanting to kill the boy for the hurt he had done her in his coming. And the other one was crying out to us to save her from that.

I tried to take a step forward but the wind got up again and pushed me back, like a blow on the chest. I lost sight of the children in the spray. Merlyn held on to my arm and murmured in my ear.

'Speak to her, Gwennol. You are the only one here she loves.'

Yes, Emrys Merlyn asking me for help.

It's gone long past that, I thought, thanks to you. Precious little sign of love she's shown to me or anyone else these last nine months. But I had to try. I loved both those poor children, may Lord Gorlois forgive me for it.

'Come along with me to your bed, my lover. He's only a baby. He hasn't done you any harm.'

But even before the words were out of my mouth, I knew that wasn't true. Even sleeping in her mother's belly, he'd done her and her sisters wrong.

'Uther Pendragon killed my father. And he deceived my mother. And neither of them is sorry for it. But I will make them weep.'

King Uther took a great stride into the water 'til the waves filled his boots.

'The stinking little crow!' he shouted. 'Give me my son back!'

A king's no better than the rest of the gentry that can't keep their temper. All pride and no sense. King he might be, but any shepherd-boy could have told him it was daft to come at her like that, like a wolf on a ewe-lamb. When she saw him with the water up to his waist she moved so quickly that I thought she was going to throw herself off the rock with the baby still clutched in her arms. I know I screamed.

Then Merlyn flung out his arm with the fingers of his hand spread stiff, and called down from the sky the words of power to bind her.

I'd been a fool to think his strength was going.

I hid my eyes in my hands, but I should have covered my ears. I've said a few spells myself in my time, but I've never heard words like those before, and I hope I never shall as long as I live. None of us there should have heard them spoken aloud. It froze me where I stood like a pillar of granite.

But that power held Morgan before she reached the edge of the rock. Stiff and still she grew, like his own hand pointing at her. Just the moonlight flashing in her eyes like frost.

Then our baby prince started to slip out of her arms. It seemed he was the only one the spell couldn't hold. Very slowly he dropped, like a feather falling in a dream. There wasn't one of us could move a hand to stop him. He fell straight into a pool in the hollow of the rocks. Then we saw a great wave come rolling in from the sea and carry him towards the shore.

Quick as a heron, Merlyn went diving through the swell and gathered him up in his arms, all dripping white in the moonlight. He looked down at the child for a long, still time, as if he'd waited years to hold a baby boy like that. Then he gave a great laugh that they must have heard up in Tintagel convent and tossed the boy into the sky. He caught him again, and as the next wave washed over them both he cried out, 'By the power of the old earth and the older moon and the three dark Mothers.

'By the power of the bright face of Ludd and Gwydion and Llew.'

The wind came again, and when it had passed Merlyn laughed long and merry.

'By the power of the Father and his Christ and the Spirit of Wisdom!

'I name you . . . Arthur!'

And that moment the precious mite started crying, so that we knew for sure he was alive.

I don't know why he did it, or if you could call that a Christian baptism. Did he think that Bryvyth was listening, on Tintagel Island? Or did he fear, like me, that our time might be over? I couldn't tell you if the boy was ever brought to a priest.

Then Merlyn looked hard at Uther Pendragon and said, 'You promised. He is mine for the fostering now. Britain shall not hear of this boy again until his day comes, and the land cries out to him for help.'

He came splashing back to the shore, and in three more strides he was gone into the darkness. We had none of us stirred.

I've never set eyes on the boy up to this day.

Chapter Thirty

I couldn't tell you how long we stood there without moving a muscle. Even the sea had fallen still. All of a sudden it seemed as though the charm had let us go. The waves were slapping on the pebbles again, but lower now. All the men were running about at the water's edge, clattering and shouting, as if the pair of them weren't gone beyond finding. We'd lost them both, and more besides.

And it was only then I thought to look for Morgan. Dear forgive me, if I hadn't forgotten her like those others, for the sake of her little baby brother with a face on him like the sun. I was mortally afraid she'd be gone too, drowned deep under the water at last. But she was still there, standing on that high rock with her arms empty. She hadn't moved. I never saw a creature look so lonely, old or young, as that little maid of nine years old.

Next moment Uther came to his senses and went splashing through the waves out to the rock. She didn't fight him now, not even when he grabbed her round the waist. He carried her back and threw her on the shingle at my feet. She caught at my skirt, but she wasn't clinging to me for love, the way she had that morning on the causeway when her heart broke. She was cold and shivering, but when the moonlight fell on her I saw she wasn't crying. Her little white

227

face was as tight and stern as any warrior's.

She hauled herself up to her feet, and it struck me then that she was getting as tall as I was. She looked into that blowing darkness where Merlyn had gone, and she spoke more coldly than any child you ever heard.

'He thinks now he has power over me. But he is not as wise as he believes. A woman could take his power away from him. And then the turn of Gorlois's daughters will come.'

I tried to put my arms round her, but she was stiff as ice. And I looked the way she had, to where I'd last seen Merlyn's back. You fool of a man, I cursed him. And worse than that. I took you for the wisest man in Britain. You had the power to charm her hurt away, though it was you that began it. But in the end you've no more sense than the king here. All you've done is turn her hate from him to you. And there'll be many will pay dearly for that before it's ended.

She lifted her face to me.

'Gwennol,' she said. And there was a little sob in her voice. 'Where is he? Where has Merlyn taken him?'

'I don't know, my pretty,' I told her. 'Somewhere where we'll never find him 'til he's a grown man.'

Uther Pendragon was marching back up the gully, without a thought for us. Then he stopped and turned, and he bellowed at us for all the world to hear, even the nuns if they were awake at their prayers.

'Get rid of that little hell-cat, once and for all! Take her to Tintagel tomorrow and shut her in the nunnery! And let me not set eyes on her again 'til those women have schooled the wickedness out of her black heart, or I swear I'll take off her head with my own sword!'

And so I lost my baby.

They sent Morgan to school with the nuns at

Tintagel. Though I could have told Uther Pendragon what else she might learn there, if only he'd taken the trouble to ask me. The air was sweet with the singing of psalms in the daytime. But there was that done in the dark place beneath that you wouldn't find in any Christian gospel. Not that Morgan needed anyone to teach her.

There was a scandal when it was found out. It broke Bryvyth's heart. The white nuns have been swept away from Tintagel now. The men have got it for themselves, as they always wanted. Though in the end it wasn't Gorlois who built his stronghold where the two currents meet.

That was years ago. Gorlois's daughters are grown into three tall queens now. Three handsome, wise women, each married to her king. You know the rest as well as I do. Uther Pendragon is dead, poisoned by his enemies, and Ygerne has taken holy vows.

Those white women weren't the only ones swept away. They're still in Cornwall somewhere, clinging to their rocks like gulls. We're not rid of them yet. But in the east the news is worse. That white dragon Merlyn dreamed of is growing fatter every day. There's many a priest and nun won't see another Easter. And many a brave British boy that's food for the Raven. The whole land's in danger now.

And so they say our little Arthur has come again and found his sword.

Well, there you have it. I've done my story, and now I'll tell you why. Morgan herself is here tonight, waiting outside that door. And she's come calling us to help her right her wrongs. So, my sisters, I'll put it to you. What shall we wise women do about the Pendragon's son?